GOTHIC NOVELS

GOTHIC NOVELS

Advisory Editor:
Dr. Sir Devendra P. Varma

THE BRAVO
OF VENICE

A ROMANCE

Translated by
M. G. LEWIS

Introduction by Davendra P. Varma

ARNO PRESS
*A New York Times Company
in cooperation with*
McGRATH PUBLISHING COMPANY
New York—1972

PT
2591
.Z32
A2
1972x

Reprint Edition 1972 by Arno Press Inc.

Special Contents Copyright © 1972 by Devendra P. Varma

LC# 74-131327
ISBN 0-405-00807-4

Gothic Novels
ISBN for complete set: 0-405-00800-7
See last page of this volume for titles.

Manufactured in the United States of America

This edition of
The Bravo of Venice
is dedicated to MARIO PRAZ
with admiration for his genius
and gratitude for his many kindnesses

Introduction

*I would give many a Sugar Cane
Monk Lewis were alive again!*
—*Byron.*

A sombre account of a singular funereal episode is contained in the pages of the log-book of the vessel *Sir Godfrey Webster,* the ship which Monk Lewis had boarded on May 4th, 1818, on his final homeward voyage to England from Jamaica. He was accompanied and attended by his favourite Venetian valet Baptista or Tita, who had previously been Byron's gondolier. It is recorded that the voyage had been rough and stormy, and soon after, Lewis already in failing health, suffered an attack of yellow fever. Most of the time he had been sea-sick and uneasy, restless and irritable, racked with a morbid bodily condition consequent to an undue rise of temperature and pulse. He had developed serious symptoms on the night of May 13th and was suffering from a terrible delirium. The attention of the Captain was called by the lookout men; the ship's engines were slowed down at his command. And as the garish dawn broke over the turbulent waters of the Atlantic, approximately at 4 a.m., Monk Lewis passed away in sleep in the arms of his faithful Tita.

The same day a coffin was manufactured on board the ship. The dismal Burial Service, as appointed in the Book of Common Prayer, was solemnly read by Captain Boyes, while the ship's inmates stood in mute silence. Finally the casket containing the precious body of Monk Lewis was gently lowered into the ocean tomb, only, however, to surge again upon the boisterous waves. The blowing wind and the breakers swept the hearse away in the direction of Jamaica.

Loud commands were shouted to the Quartermaster at the wheel; the ship's bells clanged. Instantaneously the ship's prow began to swing to starboard full steam ahead. Storm clouds lowered in the sky as the fore-foot of the ship cut through the dark waters. And before one could realize, the coffin was fading away in the distance, a tiny speck drifting on some strange current, growing fainter and fainter to view, receding and still receding till nothing but a spot remained on the far horizon finally disappearing as a mist or smoke under a breeze.

Matthew Gregory Lewis, the high-priest of gothic romance, was born in London in 1775, in an opulent family, the eldest son of Matthew Lewis, Deputy Secretary of War, who owned an ancient home and a fine estate in Surrey. On the death of his father in 1812 he succeeded to a handsome patrimony, part of which consisted of an extensive West Indian property.

Towards the close of 1815, Lewis made his first visit to Jamaica to investigate the condition of about 500 slaves who were employed upon his estate. He has left a most charming and graphic record of his impressions and experiences in his *Journal of a West India Proprietor* (1834).

It is a curious coincidence in literary history that in 1796 Lewis was returned to Parliament from Hindon in Wiltshire, a constituency which had earlier been represented by William Beckford of Fonthill, the author of *Vathek*. It is purely coincidental, yet strange, that this parliamentary seat was held by two reputed authors in succession who had so much in common: Beckford, in his youth, had earned fame as the author of *Vathek*, and Lewis had made his mark with *The Monk*. Beckford's source of fabulous income derived from the West Indies; Lewis also inherited large states in Jamaica. And again, both had got weary of Parliament and retired from it.

Slenderly built and softly reared, Lewis was of an imaginative bent and a curiously sensitive mind. In stature he was small but well formed; his countenance was expressive and manner gentlemanly; and his conversation was reported to be pleasant and kindly. Even as a child he had shown a strange predilection for the marvellous and the supernatural. Like young Shelley haunting the graveyards, Lewis also had played with candles and phosphorent lights.

As 'Monk' Lewis lay dying in the dismal cabin of the Atlantic steamer, looking through the port-hole, his delirious brain conjured up visions of the past. Old memories and half-forgotten dreams surged in his mind. He remembered his mother, Francis Maria, the handsome daughter of Sir Thomas Sewell, a woman of remarkable beauty whose absorption with the supernatural had a great impact upon her son.

He went on to think how tall and graceful his mother had been, how respected and admired by everybody, the mistress who maintained the dignity of the great edifice, the Stanstead Hall in Essex, a very ancient mansion and family seat, where Lewis's childhood was spent. He remembered the spacious garden, the nectarines and peaches hung upon the walls, and the old melancholy looking yew trees and the firs throwing their dark shadows on the moonlit turf. As a child he had roamed about the grounds sometimes reclining upon the green grass with all the fresh garden smells to envelope him.

Through his tearful eyes he could envision the face of his mother and recall her love of music and books and the quiet joys of social life interspersed with modest entertainments. The remembrance of Stanstead Hall revived wistful memories of the dewy freshness of spring mornings and langorous summer afternoons with tea served upon the velvet meadow, the autumn rambles in the tinted groves, the solemn winter evenings with the drawn purple blinds, and the beautiful blaze of fire in the grate.

He remembered how his mother used to sleep by herself in a solitary chamber of that great lone house adorned with its age-old hangings, fluttering tapestry, and carved oaken panels, and how she believed that an apparition was to be seen at midnight in the corridor below the great landing staircase.

Indeed, a certain wing of the Hall had long remained in disuse and shuttered, owing to reported ghostly hauntings, in particular, one magnificent apartment called the "Cedar Room" which no domestic could dare visit after the fall of dusk. Sudden impressions and memories of its huge and strangely carved doors, its large landing and intricate workmanship upon the chimney-piece, came back once again to his failing consciousness. He remembered how as a child while being taken to bed at night, as the moon-beam stole palely through the painted oriel upon the sombre portals, the old portraits on the walls seemed to live again. How frightened he used to be, and with a quick glance of terror over his shoulder, he would hasten his steps, clinging closer to his companion's hand lest the doors should part asunder and there glide in some ghastly phantom of the dark, some bleeding apparition or a skeleton in clanking chains. Such memories were to be absorbed in many striking episodes of *The Castle Spectre*. But the character of the house was in itself a Romance.

Pictures of the past flashed across his mind once again, like dying embers in an extinguishing fire. He indulged in reminiscence of his continental tours, his visit to Byron and Shelley, and the experience of many spectral nights: how he had been a welcome guest and a frequent visitor at the ghostly soirées at the Villa Diodati in Geneva during 1816. He recalled the storm-laden clouds lowering upon the waters of the Lake and thunders rumbling upon the mountain peaks while jagged lightnings forked across a sombre sky. He mused on those glacial mountains mantled in bristling pine and piercing the clear air and the falling shadows of the evening. He remembered the penetrating gaze of Claire Clairmont, Mary Shelley's half-sister and Byron's mistress. He was haunted by the old, familiar faces: handsome Byron, Walter Scott and spirited Shelley.

In the summer of 1792, he remembered, when just seventeen, he had taken residence in Weimer to acquire proficiency in the German language. The city, then was a seat of famous literary celebrities like Schiller, Herder, Wieland, and he was introduced to Goethe the celebrated author of *Werther*. Lewis's sojourn in Weimer was to wield a lasting influence upon his whole life; it moulded his taste, directed his interests and shaped his literary style. He caught the passion for the *marvellous,* in Germany, acquired a mastery of the German tongue, and as Scott once remarked, Lewis "wasted himself on ghost-stories and German romances". On the way back from Weimer, Lewis on his first visit to Scotland had sojourned at Bothwell Castle, the seat of Lord Douglas.

On his return to Oxford in February 1793, Lewis

translated Schiller. In the following year he was deputed as an attaché at the British Embassy in the Hague. He found the city dull; but the terrible ennui and boredom of the place seemed to have provided a literary stimulus. In a letter to his mother, dated the 18th May 1794, Lewis related that he was working on a romance, having been inspired by reading *The Mysteries of Udolpho,* which in his opinion was "one of the most interesting books ever published". Later, on the 22nd July 1794, he noted that he found nothing in the world to do in the bland life of The Hague. He did not find a single soul with whom he could converse, nor any society of any sort or kind. In fact, he eagerly awaited his recall to Britain.

The Monk was written when Lewis was only twenty. In a span of ten weeks, he produced the script, and confessed in September 1794 that "I am so much pleased with it that, if the booksellers will not buy it, I shall publish it myself".

The first edition of *The Monk* (summer 1795, London, according to Montague Summers) was a maiden production which immediately obtained rapid and extensive celebrity. It resounded with both success and scandal. It took its place with pornography, and even a century after its appearance, it was spoken of as a lewd book. Although this romance was at once severely assailed by the reviewers on grounds of immorality, its popularity never diminished nonetheless.

The critics who assailed it on the score of its immorality, further censured it for want of originality. The *Monthly Review* of June 1797 thus commented:

> The outline of Ambrosio's story was suggested by that of the 'Santon Barsisa' in the *Guardian;* the form of temptation is borrowed from that in *The Devil in Love,* by Canzotte; and the catastrophe is taken from

The Sorcerer. The adventures of Raymond and Agnes are less obviously imitations; yet the forest scene near Strasburg brings to mind an incident in Smollett's *Ferdinand Count Fathom;* the bleeding nun is described by the author as a popular tale of the Germans; and the convent prison resembles the inflictions of Mrs. Radcliffe.

In this context it may be noted that the episode of the Bleeding Nun is a tradition still credited in many parts of Germany, and it has been told that the ruins of the Castle of Lauenstein, which she is supposed to haunt, may still be visited upon the borders of Thuringia.

However, the *London Review* of February 1797 called *The Monk,* "a singular composition" which despite the lack of originality, morals, or probability to recommend it, had excited the curiosity of the public. It complimented "the irresistible energy of the genius" of Monk Lewis. *The Critical Review* discovered in him "an imagination rich, powerful and fervid".

The Monk remains a tale of a diabolical assault upon a virtuous man by a wily temptress, a crafty spirit in female shape, where the diabolical forces are brought in stronger colours and in a quick succession of kaleidoscopic pictures. It contains a plot well conceived and ingeniously worked out. *The Analytical Review* of 1796 remarked that "the whole temptation is artfully contrived".

Lewis, as the author of this novel, soon turned into a literary celebrity. The very fact that he rose to the reputation of being addressed as "Monk Lewis"—a patronymic, which foreigners regarded as his actual name—appears to be in itself a plenteous testimony of the impression made by this notorious exemplar of gothic romance.

In 1804 was published *The Bravo of Venice,* the most popular of Lewis's lesser works. Its brief dedication to the *Earl of Moira* is dated from Inverary Castle, October 27th, 1804. It ran into a fifth edition by 1807, and had the distinction of being the first number of *The Romancist and Novelists' Library,* 1839. There were constant reprints of this novel until the end of the century.

Montague Summers has commented that in some of the later editions the form of the story got slightly altered, and despite the fact that some minor details were closely knit to quicken the pace of events, the narrative could hardly gain any further improvement. *The Critical Review* of July 1805, attempted a detailed examination of this novel in an article spread over several pages. It categorized this work as a "Germanico-terrific Romance" and suggested that one "should peruse its contents with unruffled attention though our solitary chamber should be lighted by the glimmering of a single taper". Although Lewis had confessed that it was a romance translated from the German of Zschokke's *Abaellino, der grosse Bandit* (1794), the reviewer was not acquainted with the original work, but from the quality and spirit of the performance, he categorically stated that "the German author had lost nothing by this change of dress". Impressed by the startling and terrific scenes of wonders he added that "Mr. Lewis possesses a fertile imagination and considerable genius; we would therefore advise him to quit the beaten track of imitation".

The narrative of *The Bravo of Venice* is engrossing, the language has an animated glow, while the *denouement* is breath-taking and exciting. It would perhaps be unfair to present any analysis of the plot, as the mysteries of the tale would be undermined and "the reader would be deprived of the pleasure which results from astonishment". The reviewer was positive that this author "stands in the predicament of a conjuror, who would lose his power of exciting admiration, if his tricks were previously explained". As a specimen of entertainment "the turn up and turn down of every leaf introduces the hero in a new situation, and creates fresh matter for surprise and wonder". Commenting upon the quality of character presentation, the reviewer said: "Perhaps the nursery of our author was ornamented with those pictures of the gentleman and the lady, where half of each figure is in full dress, while the other half of each is a naked skeleton; and this may account for this perpetual introduction of characters, which are creatures partly of this world and partly of another".

The Critical Review was very discerning, but complimentary on the genius and contribution of 'Monk' Lewis:

> Novels have commonly been divided into the pathetic, the sentimental, and the humorous; but the writers of the German school have introduced a new class, which may be called *electric*. Every chapter contains a shock; and the reader not only stares, but starts, at the close of every paragraph; so that we cannot think the wit of a brother-critic far-fetched, when he compared the shelf in his library, on which the Tales of Wonder, the Venetian Bravo, and other similar productions were piled, to a galvanic battery.

Admiring the quality of its workmanship, Harris of Covent Garden urged Lewis to dramatize this work. Consequently its stage version appeared as *Rugantino; or the Bravo of Venice,* which, reportedly, was a thundering success at the theatre.

A passing reference may be made of *Feudal Tyrants* (1806), another excellently told romance by 'Monk' Lewis. There had already been enough of ghastly visages, crawling worms, death's heads and crossbones, but here in *Feudal Tyrants* Lewis gave a "fresh-wrought tissue of blood and murder". *The Critical Review* of July 1807 noted that "of blood, vengeance, and misfortunes Mr. Lewis has indeed woven a formidable web, but not a ghost flits along the corner of a ruined hall or draws the curtain at the dead of night to delight the old or terrify the timid fair. . . . To take ghosts and devils from Mr. Lewis's tales is to endanger their very existence". Lewis had ransacked the repositories of German literature; indeed, all the German gothic ingredients like "ghosts, bones, chains, dungeons, castles, forests, murders, and rapine pass before us in long order".

Lewis was also the author of several grand-romantic-melodramas, the most famous being *The Castle Spectre* (1798). This play is a work of genius, a wonderful phantasmagoria of the supernatural, demons, witches, dragons, giants, set amid desolate hills and gloomy cascades or sinister castle halls, all illuminated by flashes of lightning or heralded by crashing thunders, and we witness scenes of sacrifice of human victims at the altar of the Powers of Darkness. In fact, Lewis unfolds a whole arsenal of the mythical mystery of the Tales of Terror and displays gruesome imagination and gory dramatic power. He possessed histrionic talents of a high order, and there had been regrets expressed in many quarters that Matthew did not adopt the stage as a career.

There had been two different and distinctive constellations in the gothic galaxy: one with Radcliffe as the central planet and a ring of her imitator satellites, the other with Lewis as the high-priest of *Schauerroman* surrounded by his appendant proselytes. These two constellations are of different magnitude, texture and brilliance. There is Radcliffe hung in her soft splendour in the sky, and far in the horizon may be seen 'Monk' Lewis blazoning like a bright comet with its luminous trail.

Both had inspired a swarm of imitators who pirated and pilfered their themes, characters and incidents, which were often counterfeited with exemplary fidelity; even in dialogue and style there appeared very distinct verbal echoes. Yet there remains a wide range of qualitative difference between the works of Mrs. Radcliffe and Lewis. They stand on common ground with regard to their material and certain romantic subject matter, but they are entirely contrary in their individual methods of approach and treatment of the subject. Both operate and wield picturesque properties, set their scenes in convents and castles, or use the machinery of the Holy Office; but Lewis could not minister to Radcliffe's use of suspense or sensibility, nor to those landscape paintings which scintillate and illumine some of her loveliest passages.

Mrs. Radcliffe is the romanticist of the gothic novel, her terrors were more spiritual. Lewis is a perspicacious realist who in his violence and impassioned realism is widely separated from Mrs. Radcliffe and her followers. Certainly, *The Mysteries of Udolpho* had impressed him, but he carried his methods beyond the artistic reticence of Radcliffe. The author of *Udolpho* quailed at the nefarious demonism of Lewis; his scenes of matricide, incest, and rape, overwhelmed her; she never did accept his whiffs from the charnel house and festering relics of decay. Radcliffe represents the artistic, delicate and sensitive aspect of "English" gothicism, while Lewis remains the champion of the diabolic and Mephistophelian "German" *Schauerroman*.

His strangely chequered career interspersed with extremely fortunate adventures, his gothic romances, ballads of the macabre and melodramatic plays—all displaying a very lively imagination and a great turn of the narrative—had led to an early recognition of Lewis's genius, but his works suffered the undying spite of the reviewers.

Lewis unleashed a powerful and imaginative force which energized and inspired numerous novels. With all his shortcomings Lewis was an accomplished scholar gifted with an unbounded fancy. Often morbid and wayward, yet his vital and compelling power had an illimitable influence upon the gothic movement. Such sensational works of fiction like *The Black Monk,* or *The Secret of the Great Turret* (1844) by Thomas Presket Prest, and *The Monk of Udolpho* (1807) by T. J. Horsley-Curties owe much to *The Monk.*

His enthusiasm touched a responsive chord in Shelley and Byron, Coleridge and Scott. When Lewis had visited Edinburgh in 1798, Scott was then quite unknown in the literary world. Scott bore a real affection for his amiable and eccentric friend who gave him great encouragement in the early years of his writing. He thought very highly of the genius of Lewis.

Byron, while paying his tribute in *English Bards and Scotch Reviewers,* called him "wonder-working Lewis" who fain would make Parnassus a church-yard, the "Apollo's Sexton" whose brow be adorned not with laurel but with "wreaths of yew".

Dalhousie University   *Devendra P. Verma*
Nova Scotia

Select Bibliography

I GENERAL

Birkhead, Edith. *The Tale of Terror.* 1921.
Railo, Eino. *The Haunted Castle.* 1927.
Tompkins, J. M. S. *The Popular Novel in England (1770-1800).* 1932.
Praz, Mario. *The Romantic Agony.* 1933.
Summers, Montague. *The Gothic Quest.* 1938.
Varma, Devendra P. *The Gothic Flame.* 1957.

II SPECIAL

Baron-Wilson, Cornwell. *The Life and Correspondence of M. G. Lewis.* 2 vols. 1839.
Rentsch, Max. *Matthew Gregory Lewis. Mit besonderer berucksichtigung seines Romans 'Ambrosio, or The Monk'.* 1902.
Guthke, Karl S. *Englishe Vorromantic und Deutscher Sturm and Drang.* 1958.
Parreaux, Andre. *The Publication of The Monk.* 1960.

THE
BRAVO OF VENICE,
A Romance:

TRANSLATED FROM THE GERMAN

BY M. G. LEWIS.

What black magician conjures up this fiend?—
What! do ye tremble? are ye all afraid?
Alas! I blame you not, for ye are mortal,
And mortal eyes cannot endure the Devil—
Avaunt! thou dreadful Minister of Hell!

RICHARD THE THIRD.

LONDON:
Printed by D. N. SHURY, No. 7, Berwick Street, Soho,
FOR J. F. HUGHES, WIGMORE STREET,
CAVENDISH SQUARE.

1805.

TO

THE EARL OF MOIRA

These pages are inscribed, as a slight mark of that respect for his character and conduct, which [though felt in common with many] is felt more sensibly by none than by

His most obedient,

M. G. LEWIS.

Inveraray Castle,
October 27th, 1804.

ADVERTISEMENT.

I must confess, that in making this translation I have taken some liberties with the original—Every thing that relates to Monaldeschi [a personage who does not exist in the German romance] and the whole of the concluding chapter [with the exception of a very few sentences] have been added by myself. I have also omitted a song, supposed to be sung by Rosabella, in the fourth chapter of the third book, the merit of which I could not discover; and several passages, which seemed to me too harsh for the taste of English readers, have been either left out entirely, or considerably softened down. However, where the expressions appeared to be either characteristic of the author's style, or of the character by whom they were supposed to be used, I did not think myself at liberty to alter them; I have therefore suffered Parozzi's speech in the third book about " the devil's grandmother," as well as several others, to remain, though I request not to be supposed to have retained them in compliment to my own taste.

THE TRANSLATOR.

CONTENTS.

BOOK THE FIRST.

Chap. 1. *Venice* .... *Page* 1
Chap. 2. *The Banditti* 12
Chap. 3. *The trial of strength* 23
Chap. 4. *The Daggers* 36
Chap. 5. *Solitude* 48
Chap. 6. *Rosabella, the Doge's lovely Niece* 57
Chap. 7. *The Bravo's Bride* 71
Chap. 8. *The Conspiracy* 78
Chap. 9. *Cinthia's dwelling* 98

BOOK THE SECOND.

Chap. 1. *The Birthday* ...... *Page* 116
Chap. 2. *The Florentine Stranger*....141
Chap. 3. *More confusion* 161
Chap. 4. *The Violet*................172
Chap. 5. *The Assassin*..............194
Chap. 6. *The two greatest men in Venice*................206

BOOK THE THIRD.

Chap. 1. *The Lovers* 220
Chap. 2. *A dangerous promise*.......235
Chap. 3. *The midnight meeting*......259
Chap. 4. *The decisive day* 272
Chap. 5. *The clock strikes " Five!"*..286
Chap. 6. *Apparitions!* 301
Chap. 7. *Conclusion* 337

THE
BRAVO OF VENICE.

Translated from the German.

BOOK THE FIRST

CHAP. I.

Venice.

It was evening——Multitudes of light clouds, partially illumined by the moon-beams, overspread the horizon, and through them floated the full moon in tranquil majesty, while her splendour was reflected by every wave of the Adriatic Sea. All was hushed around; gently was the water rippled by the night-wind; gently did the night-wind sigh through the Colonnades of Venice.

It was midnight——and still sat a stranger, solitary and sad, on the border of the great Canal. Now with a glance he measured the battlements and proud towers of the city; and now he fixt his melancholy eyes upon the waters with a vacant stare. At length he spoke.

—" Wretch that I am, whither shall I go? Here sit I in Venice, and what would it avail to wander further?— What will become of me! All now slumber, save myself! the Doge rests on his couch of down; the beggar's head

head presses his straw-pillow; but for *me* there is no bed, except the cold damp earth! there is no Gondoleer so wretched, but he knows where to find work by day, and shelter by night— while *I.* . . . while *I.* . . . Oh! dreadful is the destiny, of which I am made the sport!"—

He began to examine for the twentieth time the pockets of his tattered garments.

—" No! not one paolo, by heavens! —and I hunger almost to death!"—

He unsheathed his sword; he waved it in the moonshine, and sighed, as he marked the glittering of the steel.

—" No, no! my old and true companion, thou and I must never part! Mine thou shalt remain, though I starve for it.—Oh! was not that a golden time, when Valeria gave thee to me, and when as she threw the belt over my shoulder, I kist thee and Valeria?—She has deserted us for another world; but thou and I will never part in this."—

He wiped away a drop, which hung upon his eye-lid.

—" Psha! 'twas not a tear! the night-wind is sharp and bitter, and makes the eyes water; but as for *tears*.... Absurd! my weeping-days are over."—

And as he spoke, the unfortunate [for such by his discourse and situation he appeared

appeared to be] dashed his forehead against the earth, and his lips were already unclosed to curse the hour which gave him being, when he suddenly seemed to recollect himself. He rested his head on his elbow, and sang mournfully the burthen of a song, which had often delighted his childhood in the castle of his ancestors.

—" Right!" he said to himself; " Were I to sink under the weight of my destiny, I should be myself no longer."—

At that moment he heard a rustling at no great distance. He looked around, and in an adjacent street, which the moon faintly enlightened, he perceived a tall figure wrapt in a cloak, pacing slowly backwards and forwards.

—" 'Tis the hand of God, which hath guided him hither—Yes!—I'll—I'll *beg!*—Better to play the beggar in Venice, than the villain in Naples; for the beggar's heart may beat nobly though covered by rags!"—

He said, sprang from the ground, and hastened towards the adjoining street. Just as he entered it at one end, he perceived another person advancing through the other, of whose approach the first was no sooner aware, than he hastily retired into the shadow of a piazza, as anxious to conceal himself.

—" What

—" What can this mean ?" thought our mendicant. " Is yon eaves-dropper one of death's unlicensed ministers? Has he received the retaining-fee of some impatient heir, who pants to possess the wealth of the unlucky knave, who comes strolling along yonder so careless and unconscious?—Be not so confident, honest friend! I'm at your elbow.'—

He retired further into the shade, and silently and slowly drew near the lurker, who stirred not from his place. The stranger had already passed them by, when the concealed villain sprang suddenly upon him, raised his right hand in which a poignard was gleaming, and before he could give the blow, was

felled

felled to the earth by the arm of the mendicant.

The stranger turned hastily towards them; the Bravo started up, and fled; the beggar smiled.

—" How now ?" cried the stranger; " What does all this mean ?"—

—" Oh! 'tis a mere jest, Signor, which has only preserved your life."—

—" What? My life? How so?"—

" The honest gentleman, who has just taken to his heels, stole behind you with true cat-like caution, and had already raised his dagger, when I saw him

him—You owe your life to me, and the service is richly worth one little piece of money! Give me some alms, Signor, for on my soul I am hungry, thirsty, cold!"—

—" Hence, scurvy companion! I know you, and your tricks too well. This is all a concerted scheme between you, a design upon my purse, an attempt to procure both money and thanks under the lame pretence of having saved me from an assassin.—Go, fellow, go! practise these dainty devices on the Doge's credulity, if you will; but with Buonarotti you stand no chance, believe me."—

The wretched starving beggar stood like one petrified, and gazed on the taunting stranger.

—" No,

—" No, as I have a soul to save, Signor, 'tis no lye that I tell you!—'tis the plain truth; have compassion, or I die this night of hunger."—

—" Begone this instant, I say, or by heaven...."—

The unfeeling man here drew out a concealed pistol, and pointed it at his preserver.

—" Merciful Heaven! and is it thus that services are acknowledged in Venice?"—

—" The watch is at no great distance; I need only raise my voice, and ...."—

—" Hell

—" Hell and confusion! Do you take me for a robber then?"—

—" Make no noise, I tell you! Be quiet, you had better!"—

—" Hark you, Signor! Buonarotti is your name, I think? I will write it down, as belonging to the second scoundrel with whom I have met in Venice."—

He paused for a moment; then continuing in a dreadful voice,—" And when," said he, " thou, Buonarotti, shalt hereafter hear the name of *Abellino......tremble!"*—

Abellino turned away, and left the hard-hearted Venetian.

CHAP. II.

The Banditti.

And now rushed the unfortunate wildly through the streets of Venice; he railed at fortune; he laughed and cursed by turns; yet sometimes he suddenly stood still, seemed as pondering on some great and wond'rous enterprize, and then again rushed onwards, as if hastening to its execution.

Propped against a column of the Signoria, he counted over the whole sum
of

of his misfortunes. His wandering eyeballs seemed to seek comfort; but they found it not.

—" Fate," he at length exclaimed in a paroxysm of despair, " Fate has condemned me to be either the wildest of adventurers.... or one, at the relation of whose crimes the world must shudder! To astonish is my destiny: Rosalvo can know no medium: Rosalvo can never act like common men!—Is it not the hand of fate, which has led me hither? Who could have ever dreamt, that the son of the richest Lord in Naples should have depended for a beggar's alms on Venetian charity! *I.... I,* who feel myself possest of strength of body and energy of soul fit for executing the most daring deeds.... Behold me creeping in

rags

rags through the streets of this inhospitable city, and torturing my wits in vain to discover some means, by which I may rescue life from the jaws of famine! Those men, whom my munificence nourished, who at my table bathed their worthless souls in the choicest wine of Cyprus, and glutted themselves with every delicacy which the globe's four quarters could supply, those very men now deny to my necessity even a miserable crust of mouldy bread.—Oh! that is dreadful, cruel! Cruel of men! cruel of Heaven!"—

He paused; he folded his arms, and sighed.

—" Yet will I bear it! I will submit to my destiny! I will traverse every path,

path, and go through every degree of human wretchedness; and whate'er may be my fate, I will be still *myself*, and whate'er may be my fate, I will still act *greatly!*——Away then with the Count Rosalvo, whom once all Naples idolized: now.... now am I the *beggar Abellino!* —A beggar?—that name stands *last* in the scale of worldly rank, but *first* in the list of the famishing, the outcast, and the unworthy."—

Something rustled near him—Abellino gazed around. He was aware of the Bravo, whom he had struck to the ground that night, and whom two companions of a similar stamp had now joined. As they advanced, they cast inquiring glances around them. They were in search of some one.

—" It

—" It is of *thee*, that they are in search," said Abellino, then advanced a few steps, and whistled.

The ruffians stood still—they whispered together, and seemed to be undecided.

Abellino whistled a second time.

—" 'Tis he!"—could he hear one of them say distinctly—and in a moment after they advanced slowly towards him.

Abellino kept his place, but unsheathed his sword. The three unknown [they were masked] stopped a few paces from him.

—" How now, fellow?" quoth one
of

of them, " What is the matter? Why stand you on your guard?"—

Abellino.—" It is as well that you should be made to keep your distance, for I *know* you; you are certain honest gentlemen, who live by taking away the lives of others."—

The First Ruffian—Was not your whistling addrest to *us?*

Abellino—It was.

A Ruffian—And what would you with us?

Abellino—Hear me! I am a miserable wretch, and starving; give me an alms out of your booty!

A Ruffian

A Ruffian—An alms ? Ha! ha! ha!
By my soul, that is whimsical!—Alms
from us, indeed!—Oh! by all means!
No doubt, you shall have alms in plenty!

Abellino—Or else give me fifty sequins, and I'll bind myself to your service, till I shall have worked out my debt.

A Ruffian—Aye? And pray then, who may you be?

Abellino—A starving wretch, the republic holds none more miserable. Such am I *at present*; but hereafter.... I have powers, knaves.... this arm could pierce an heart, though guarded by three breastplates; this eye, though surrounded
ed

ed by Egyptian darkness, could still see to stab sure.

A Ruffian—Why then did you strike me down even now?

Abellino—In the hope of being paid for it; but though I saved his life, the scoundrel gave me not a single ducat.

A Ruffian—No? So much the better. —But hark ye, comrade! are you sincere?

Abellino—Despair never lyes.

A Ruffian—Slave, shouldst thou be a traitor....

Abellino—My heart would be within

reach of your hands, and your daggers would be as sharp as now.

The three dangerous companions again whispered among themselves for a few moments, after which they returned their daggers into the sheath.

—" Come on then," said one of them; " Follow us to our home. It were unwise to talk over certain matters in the open street."—

—" I follow you," was Abellino's answer; " But tremble, should any one of you dare to treat me as a foe.—Comrade, forgive me that I gave your ribs somewhat too hard a squeeze just now; I will be your sworn brother in recompense."—

—" We

—" We are on honour," cried the banditti with one voice, " No harm shall happen to you: he, who does *you* an injury, shall be to *us* as a foe. A fellow of your humour suits us well: follow us, and fear not."—

And on they went, Abellino marching between two of them. Frequent were the looks of suspicion, which he cast around him; but no ill design was perceptible in the banditti. They guided him onwards, till they reached a canal, loosened a gondola, placed themselves in it, and rowed, till they had gained the most remote quarter of Venice. They landed, threaded several bye-streets, and at length knocked at the door of an house of inviting appearance—It was opened by a young woman, who conducted them

them into a plain but comfortable chamber; many were the looks of surprize and enquiry which she cast on the bewildered half-pleased half-anxious Abellino, who knew not whither he had been conveyed, and still thought it unsafe to confide entirely in the promises of the banditti.

CHAP. III.

The trial of strength.

Scarcely were the bravos seated, when Cinthia [for that was the young woman's name] was again summoned to the door; and the company was now increased by two new-comers, who examined their unknown guest from head to foot.

—" Now then," cried one of those, who had conducted Abellino to this respectable society, " Let us see, what you are like."—

As he said this, he raised a burning lamp from the table, and the light of its flame was thrown full upon Abellino's countenance.

—" Lord, forgive me my sins!" screamed Cinthia; " Out upon him! what an ugly hound it is!"—

She turned hastily round, and hid her face with her hands. Dreadful was the look, with which Abellino repaid her compliment.

—" Knave," said one of the banditti, " Nature's own hand has marked you out for an assassin—Come, pry'thee be be frank, and tell us, how thou hast contrived so long to escape the gibbet? In what gaol didst thou leave thy last fetters? Or from what galley hast thou taken thy departure, without staying to say adieu?"—

Abellino folded his arms.

—" If I be such as you describe," said he with an air of authority and in a voice which made his hearers tremble, " 'Tis for me all the better. Whate'er may be my future mode of life, Heaven can have no right to find fault with it, since it was for that it formed and fitted me."—

The five bravos stepped aside, and consulted together; the subject of their conference

conference is easy to be divined. In the meanwhile Abellino remained quiet, and indifferent to what was passing.

After a few minutes they again approached him : one, whose countenance was the most ferocious, and whose form exhibited the greatest marks of muscular strength, advanced a few paces before the rest, and address Abellino as follows :

—" Hear me, comrade. In Venice there exist but five banditti; you see them before you; wilt thou be the sixth, doubt not, thou wilt find sufficient employment. My name is Matteo, and I am the father of the band : that sturdy fellow with the red locks is called Baluzzo; he, whose eyes twinkle like a cat's cat's, is Thomaso, an arch knave I promise you ! 'Twas Pietrino, whose bones you handled so roughly to-night; and yon thick-lipped Colossus, who stands next to Cinthia, is named Struzza. Now then you know us all—and since you are a pennyless devil, we are willing to incorporate you in our society; but we must first be assured, that you mean honestly by us."—

Abellino smiled, or rather grinned, and murmured hoarsely—" I am starving!"—

—" Answer, fellow! Dost thou mean honestly by us ?"—

—" That must the event decide."—

—" Mark

—" Mark me, knave; the first suspicion of treachery costs you your life. Take shelter in the Doge's palace, and girdle yourself round with all the power of the republic—though clasped in the Doge's arms, and protected by an hundred canons, still would we murder you! Fly to the high altar; press the crucifix to your bosom; and even at mid-day, still would we murder you! Think on this well, fellow, and forget not, we are *banditti!*"—

—" You need not tell me that——But give me some food, and then I'll prate with you, as long as you please—At present I am starving! Four and twenty hours have elapsed, since I last tasted nourishment."—

Cinthia

Cinthia now covered a small table with her best provisions, and filled several silver goblets with delicious wine.

—" If one could but look at him without disgust!" murmured Cinthia; " if he had but the appearance of something human! Satan must certainly have appeared to his mother, while she was big with him, and thence came her child into the world with such a frightful countenance! Ugh! It's an absolute mask, only that I never saw a mask so hideous!"—

Abellino heeded her not: he placed himself at the table, and ate and drank, as if he would have satisfied himself for the next six months. The banditti eyed him with looks of satisfaction, and con-
gratulated

gratulated each other on such a valuable acquisition.

If the reader is curious to know what this same Abellino was like, he must picture to himself a young stout fellow, whose limbs perhaps might have been thought not ill-formed, had not the most horrible countenance, that ever was invented by a caricaturist, or that Milton could have adapted to the ugliest of his fallen angels, entirely marred the advantages of his person. Black and shining, but long and straight, his hair flew wildly about his brown neck and yellow face. His mouth was so wide, that his gums and discoloured teeth were visible, and a kind of convulsive twist which scarcely ever was at rest, had formed its expression into an eternal grin. His eye

eye [for he had but one] was sunk deep in his head, and little more than the white of it was visible; and even that little was overshadowed by the protrusion of his dark and bushy eye-brow. In the union of his features were found collected in one hideous assemblage all the most coarse and uncouth traits, which ever had been exhibited singly in wooden cuts; and the observer was left in doubt, whether this repulsive physiognomy exprest stupidity of intellect, or maliciousness of heart, or whether it implied them both together.

—" Now then I am satisfied!" roared Abellino, and dashed the still-full goblet upon the ground.—" Speak! what would you know of me? I am ready to give you answers."—

—" The

—" The first thing," replied Matteo, " the first thing necessary is to give us a proof of your strength, for this is of material importance in our undertakings. —Are you good at wrestling?"—

—" I know not: try me."—

—" Cinthia, remove the table—Now then Abellino, which of us will you undertake? Whom among us, dost think, thou canst knock down as easy as yon poor dabbler in the art, Pietrino?"

—" Which of you?" cried Abellino; " All of you together, and half a dozen more such pitiful scoundrels!"—And he sprang from his seat, threw his sword on the table, and measured the strength of his antagonists with his single eye.

The

The banditti burst into a loud fit of laughter.

—" Now then," cried Abellino fiercely; " now then for the trial!—Why come you not on?"—

—" Fellow," replied Matteo, " take my advice; try first, what you can do with me alone, and learn what sort of men you have to manage. Think you, we are marrowless boys, or delicate Signors, who waste their strength in the embrace of harlots?"

Abellino answered him by a scornful laugh—Matteo became furious: his companions shouted aloud, and clapped their hands.

—" To

—" To business!" said Abellino; " I'm now in a right humour for sport! Look to yourselves, my lads!"—And in the same instant he collected his forces together, threw the gigantic Matteo over his head as had he been an infant, knocked Struzza down on the right hand, and Pietrino on the left, tumbled Thomaso to the end of the room head over heels, and stretched Baluzzo without animation upon the neighbouring benches.

Three minutes elapsed, ere the subdued bravos could recover themselves; loud shouted Abellino, while the astonished Cinthia gazed and trembled at the terrible exhibition.

—" By the blood of St. Januarius," cried

cried Matteo at length, rubbing his battered joints, " the fellow is our master. Cinthia, take care to give him our best chamber."—

—" He must have made a compact with the devil!" grumbled Thomaso, and forced his dislocated wrist back into its socket.

No one seemed inclined to hazard a second trial of strength. The night was far advanced, or rather the grey of morning already was visible over the sea. The banditti separated, and each retired to his chamber.

CHAP. IV.

The Daggers.

ABELLINO, this Italian Hercules, all terrible as he appeared to be, was not long a member of this society, before his companions felt towards him sentiments of the most unbounded esteem. All loved, all valued him for his extraordinary talents for a Bravo's trade, to which he seemed peculiarly adapted, not only by his wonderful strength of body, but by the readiness of his wit and his
never-

never-failing presence of mind. Even Cinthia was inclined to feel some little affection for him, but.... he really was too ugly.

Matteo [as Abellino was soon given to understand] was the captain of this dangerous troop. He was one who carried villainy to the highest pitch of refinement, incapable of fear, quick and crafty, and troubled with less conscience than a French financier. The booty and price of blood, which his associates brought in daily, were always delivered up to him; he gave each man his share, and retained no larger portion for himself, than was allotted to the others. The catalogue of those, whom he had dispatched into the other world, was already too long for him to have re-

peated

peated it: many names had slipped his memory; but his greatest pleasure in his hours of relaxation was to relate such of these murderous anecdotes as he still remembered, in the benevolent intention of inspiring his hearers with a desire to follow his example. His weapons were kept separate from the rest, and occupied a whole apartment. Here were to be found daggers of a thousand different fashions, *with* guards and *without* them; two—three—and four edged. Here were stored air-guns, pistols, and blunderbusses; poisons of various kinds and operating in various ways; garments fit for every possible disguise, whether to personate the Monk, the Jew, or the Mendicant, the Soldier, the Senator, or the Gondoleer.

One

One day he summoned Abellino to attend him in this armoury.

—" Mark me," said he; " thou wilt turn out a brave fellow, that I can see already. It is now time, that you should earn that bread for yourself, which hitherto you have owed to our bounty. —Look! Here hast thou a dagger of the finest steel; you must charge for its use by the inch. If you plunge it only one inch deep into the bosom of his foe, your employer must reward you with only one sequin: if two inches, with ten sequins; if three, with twenty; if the whole dagger, you may then name your own price.—Here is next a glass poniard; whomever this pierces, that man's death is certain.—As soon as the blow is given, you must break the dagger in the wound; the flesh will close over the point which has been broken off, and which will keep its quarters till the day of resurrection!—Lastly, observe this metallic dagger; its cavity conceals a subtile poison, which whenever you touch this spring, will immediately infuse death into the veins of him whom the weapon's point hath wounded.—Take these daggers; in giving them I present you with a capital, capable of bringing home to you most heavy and most precious interest."—

Abellino received the instruments of death, but his hand shook as it grasped them.

—" Possest of such unfailing weapons

pons, of what immense sums must your robberies have made you master!"—

—" Scoundrel!" interrupted Matteo, frowning and offended, " among us robbery is unknown. What? Dost take us for common plunderers, for mere thieves, cut-purses, house-breakers, and villains of that low miserable stamp?"—

—" Perhaps what you wish me to take you for, is something worse; for to speak openly, Matteo, villains of that stamp are contented with plundering a purse or a casket, which can easily be filled again; but that which *we* take from others is a jewel, which a man never has but once, and which once stolen can never be replaced. Are we not then a
thousand

thousand times more atrocious plunderers?"—

—" By the House at Loretto, I think you have a mind to moralize, Abellino?"—

—" Hark ye, Matteo, only one question; at the day of judgment, which think you will hold his head highest, the thief, or the assassin?"—

—" Ha! ha! ha!"

—" Think not, that Abellino speaks thus from want of resolution. Speak but the word, and I murder half the senators of Venice; but still...."—

—" Fool!

—" Fool! know, the Bravo must be above crediting the nurse's antiquated tales of vice and virtue. What is virtue! What is vice? Nothing, but such things as forms of government, custom, manners, and education have made sacred; and that which men are able to make honourable at one time, it is in their power to make dishonourable at another, whenever the humour takes them: had not the senate forbidden us to give opinions freely respecting the politics of Venice, there would have been nothing wrong in giving such opinions; and were the senate to declare that it is right to give such opinions, that which to-day is thought a crime would be thought meritorious to-morrow—Then pry'thee let us have no more of such doubts as these. We are men, as much

as

as are the Doge and his senators, and have reason as much as *they* have to lay down the law of right and wrong, and to alter the law of right and wrong, and to decree what shall be vice, and what shall be virtue."—

Abellino laughed—Matteo proceeded with increased animation.

—" Perhaps you will tell me, that our trade is *dishonourable!* And what then is the thing, called *honour!* 'Tis a word, an empty sound, a mere fantastic creature of the imagination!—Ask, as you traverse some frequented street, in what honour consists ?—the usurer will answer—' To be honourable is to be rich, and he has most honour, who can heap up the greatest quantity of sequins.'
—' By

—' By no means,' cries the voluptuary; ' honour consists in being beloved by every handsome woman, and finding no virtue proof against your attacks.'— ' How mistaken!' interrupts the general; ' to conquer whole cities, to destroy whole armies, to ruin whole provinces, *that* indeed brings *real* honour!' —The man of learning places his renown in the number of pages which he has either written, or read; the tinker, in the number of pots and kettles which he has made, or mended; the nun, in the number of *good* things which she has done, or *bad* things which she has resisted; the coquette, in the list of her admirers; the republic, in the extent of her provinces; and thus, my friend, every one thinks, that honour consists in something different from the rest—And why then

then should not the Bravo think, that honour consists in reaching the perfection of his trade, and in guiding a dagger to the heart of an enemy with unerring aim?"—

—" By my life, 'tis a pity, Matteo, that you should be a Bravo; the schools have lost an excellent teacher of philosophy!"—

—" Do you think so?—Why, the fact is thus, Abellino——I was educated in a monastery; my father was a dignified prelate in Lucca, and my mother a nun of the Ursuline order, greatly respected for her chastity and devotion.—Now, Signor, it was thought fitting, that I should apply closely to my studies; my father, good man, would fain have made me me a light of the church; but I soon found, that I was better qualified for an incendiary's torch. I followed the bent of my genius, yet count I not my studies thrown away, since they taught me more philosophy than to tremble at phantoms created by my own imagination. Follow my example, friend, and so farewell."—

CHAP. V.

Solitude.

ABELLINO had already passed six weeks in Venice, and yet [either from want of opportunity, or of inclination] he had suffered his daggers to remain idle in their sheaths. This proceeded partly from his not being as yet sufficiently acquainted with the windings and turnings, the bye-lanes and private alleys of the town; and partly because he had hitherto found no customers, whose murderous

murderous designs stood in need of his helping hand.

This want of occupation was irksome to him in the extreme: he panted for action, and was condemned to indolence.

With a melancholy heart did he roam through Venice, and numbered every step with a sigh. He frequented the public places, the taverns, gardens, and every scene which was dedicated to amusement. But no where could he find what he sought—tranquillity.

One evening, he had loitered beyond the other visitants in a public garden, situated on one of the most beautiful of the Venetian islands. He strolled from arbour to arbour, threw himself down on the sea-shore, and watched the play of the waves, as they sparkled in the moon-shine.

—" Four years ago," said he with a sigh, " just such an heavenly evening was it, that I stole from Valeria's lips the first kiss, and heard from Valeria's lips for the first time the avowal, that she loved me."—

He was silent, and abandoned himself to the melancholy recollections which thronged before his mind's eye.

Every thing around him was so calm, so silent! Not a single zephyr sighed among the blades of grass; but a storm raged in the bosom of Abellino.

—" Four

—" Four years ago could I have believed, that a time would come, when I should play the part of a Bravo in Venice! Oh! where are they flown, the golden hopes and plans of glory, which smiled upon me in the happy days of my youth?—I am a Bravo; to be a beggar were to be something better.

" When my good old father in the enthusiasm of paternal vanity so oft threw his arms around my neck, and cried—' My boy, thou wilt render the name of Rosalvo glorious!'—God, as I listened, how was my blood on fire! What thought I not, what felt I not, what that was good and great did I not promise myself to do!—The father is dead, and the son.... is a Venetian Bravo!——When my preceptors praised and admired me, and, carried away by the warmth of their feelings, clapped my shoulder, and exclaimed—' Count, thou wilt immortalize the ancient race of Rosalvo!'—Ha! in those blessed moments of sweet delirium, how bright and beauteous stood futurity before me! ——When happy in the performance of some good deed, I returned home, and saw Valeria hasten to receive me with open arms, and when, while she clasped me to her bosom, I heard her whisper— ' Oh! who could forbear to love the great Rosalvo!'—.... God! oh! God! —Away, away, glorious visions of the past! To look on you drives me mad!"—

He was again silent; he bit his lip in fury, raised one emaciated hand to heaven,

ven, and struck his forehead violently with the other.

—" An assassin.... the slave of cowards and rascals.... the ally of the greatest villains, whom the Venetian sun ever shines upon.... Such is now the great Rosalvo!—Fye! oh! fye on't!—And yet to this wretched lot hath fatality condemned me."—

Suddenly he sprang from the ground after a long silence; his eyes sparkled; his countenance was changed; he drew his breath easier.

—" Yes! by Heaven, yes! Great as Count Rosalvo, that can I be no longer; but from being great as a Venetian Bravo, what prevents me?—" Souls in bliss!"

he exclaimed, and sank on his knee, while he raised his folded hands to Heaven, as if about to pronounce the most awful oath, " Spirit of my father! Spirit of Valeria! I will not become unworthy of you! Hear me, if your ghosts are permitted to wander near me, hear me swear, that the Bravo shall not disgrace his origin, nor render vain the hopes, which soothed you in the bitterness of death! No! sure as I live, I will be the only dealer in this miserable trade, and posterity shall be compelled to honour that name, which my actions shall render illustrious."—

He bowed his forehead, till it touched the earth, and his tears flowed plenteously. Vast conceptions swelled his soul: he dwelt on wonderous views, till their extent

extent bewildered his brain; yet another hour elapsed, and he sprang from the earth to realize them!

—" I will enter into no compact against human nature with five miserable cut-throats. *Alone* will I make the republic tremble, and before eight days are flown, these murderous knaves shall swing upon a gibbet. Venice shall no longer harbour *five* banditti; *one* and *one* only shall inhabit here, and that one shall beard the Doge himself, shall watch over right and over wrong, and according as he judges, shall reward, and punish. Before eight days are flown, the state shall be purified from the presence of these outcasts of humanity, and then shall *I* stand here alone! Then must every villain in Venice, who hitherto has kept the daggers of my companions in employment, have recourse to *me :* then shall I know the names and persons of all those cowardly murderers, of all those illustrious profligates, with whom Matteo and his companions carry on the trade of blood—And then. . . . Abellino! Abellino!. . . . *that* is the name ! Hear it Venice, hear it, and tremble!"—

Intoxicated with the wildness of his hopes, he rushed out of the garden ; he summoned a Gondoleer, threw himself into the boat, and hastened to the dwelling of Cinthia, where the inhabitants already were folded in the arms of sleep.

CHAP. VI.

Rosabella, the Doge's lovely Niece.

—" Hark, comrade," said Matteo the next morning to Abellino; " to-day thou shalt make thy first step in our profession."—

—" To-day?" hoarsely murmured Abellino; " and on whom am I to show my skill?"—

—" Nay, to say truth, 'tis but a woman;

woman; but one must not give too difficult a task to a young beginner. I will myself accompany you, and see how you conduct yourself in this first trial."—

—" Hum!" said Abellino, and measured Matteo with his eye from head to foot.

—" To-day about four o'clock thou shalt follow me to Dolabella's gardens, which are situated on the south side of Venice; we must both be disguised, you understand. In these gardens are excellent baths; and after using these baths, the Doge's niece, the lovely Rosabella of Corfu, frequently walks without attendants. And then.... you conceive me?"—

—" And

—" And *you* will accompany me?"—

—" I will be a spectator of your first adventure; 'tis thus I deal by every one."—

—" And how many inches deep must I plunge my dagger?"—

—" To the hilt, boy, to the very hilt! Her death is required, and the payment will be princely; Rosabella in the grave, we are rich for life."—

Every other point was soon adjusted. Noon was now past, the clock in the neighbouring church of the Benedictines struck four, and Matteo and Abellino were already forth.

They

They arrived at the gardens of Dolabella, which that day were unusually crowded. Every shady avenue was thronged with people of both sexes; every arbour was occupied by the persons most distinguished in Venice; in every corner sighed love-sick couples, as they waited for the wished approach of twilight; and on every side did strains of vocal and instrumental music pour their harmony on the enchanted ear.

Abellino mingled with the crowd. A most respectable-looking peruke concealed the repulsive ugliness of his features; he imitated the walk and manners of a gouty old man, and supported himself by a crutch, as he walked slowly through the assembly. His habit, richly embroidered, procured for him universally

sally a good reception, and no one scrupled to enter into conversation with him respecting the weather, the commerce of the republic, or the designs of its enemies; and on none of these subjects was Abellino found incapable of sustaining the discourse.

By these means he soon contrived to gain intelligence, that Rosabella was certainly in the gardens, how she was habited, and in what quarter he was most likely to find her.

Thither he immediately bent his course; and hard at his heels followed Matteo.

Alone, and in the most retired arbour,
sat

sat Rosabella of Corfu, the fairest maid in Venice.

Abellino drew near the arbour; he tottered, as he past its entrance, like one opprest with sudden faintness, and attracted Rosabella's attention.

—" Alas! alas!" cried he, " is there no one at hand, who will take compassion on the infirmity of a poor old man!"—

The Doge's fair niece quitted the arbour hastily, and flew to give assistance to the sufferer.

—" What ails you, my good father?" she enquired in a melodious voice, and with a look of benevolent anxiety.

Abellino

Abellino pointed towards the arbour; Rosabella led him in, and placed him on a seat of turf.

—" God reward you, lady!" stammered Abellino faintly; he raised his eyes; they met Rosabella's, and a blush crimsoned his pale cheeks.

Rosabella stood in silence before the disguised assassin, and trembled with tender concern for the old man's illness; and oh! that expression of interest ever makes a lovely woman look so much *more* lovely!——She bent her delicate form over the man who was bribed to murder her, and after a while asked him in the gentlest tone—" Are you not better?"—

—" Better?"

—" Better?" stammered the deceiver with a feeble voice;—" better?—oh! yes, yes, yes!—You.... you are the Doge's niece? the noble Rosabella of Corfu?"—

—" The same, my good old man."—

—" Oh! lady.... I have somewhat to tell you.... Be on your guard.... start not.... what I would say is of the utmost consequence, and demands the greatest prudence—Ah! God, that there should live men so cruel—Lady, your life is in danger."

The maiden started back; the colour fled from her cheeks.

—" Do you wish to behold your assassin?

assassin ?—You shall not die, but if you value your life, be silent."—

Rosabella knew not what to think; the presence of the old man terrified her.

—" Fear nothing, lady, fear nothing; you have nothing to fear, while I am with you—Before you quit this arbour, you shall see the assassin expire at your feet."—

Rosabella made a movement, as would she have fled; but suddenly the person who sat beside her was no longer an infirm old man. He, who a minute before had scarcely strength to mutter out a few sentences, and reclined against the arbour trembling like an aspin, sprang up up with the force of a giant, and drew her back with one arm.

—" For the love of Heaven," she cried, " release me ! Let me fly."—

—" Lady, fear nothing; *I* protect you."—Thus said Abellino, placed a whistle at his lips, and blew it shrilly.

—" Instantly sprang Matteo from his conccalment in a neighbouring clump of trees, and rushed into the arbour. Abellino threw Rosabella on the bank of turf, advanced a few steps to meet Matteo, and plunged his dagger in his heart.

Without uttering a single cry sank the Banditti-Captain at the feet of Abellino; the death-rattle was heard in his throat, and

and after a few horrible convulsions all was over.

Now did Matteo's murderer look again towards the arbour, and beheld Rosabella half senseless, as she lay on the bank of turf.

—" Your life is safe, beautiful Rosabella," said he; " there lies the villain bleeding, who conducted me hither to murder you. Recover yourself; return to your uncle the Doge, and tell him, that you owe your life to Abellino."—

Rosabella could not speak. Trembling she stretched her arms towards him, grasped his hand, and prest it to her lips in silent gratitude.

Abellino gazed with delight and wonder on the lovely sufferer; and in such a situation who could have beheld her without emotion?—Rosabella had scarcely numbered seventeen summers; her light and delicate limbs, enveloped in a thin white garment which fell around her in a thousand folds; her blue and melting eyes, whence beamed the expression of purest innocence; her forehead, white as ivory, overshadowed by the ringlets of her bright dark hair; cheeks, whence terror had now stolen the roses; lips, which a seducer had never poisoned with his kisses; such was Rosabella, a creature in whose formation partial Nature seemed to have omitted nothing, which might constitute the perfection of female loveliness—Such was she; and being such, the wretched Abellino may be forgiven,

forgiven, if for some few minutes he stood like one enchanted, and bartered for those few minutes the tranquillity of his heart for ever.

—" By Him who made me," cried he at length, " oh! thou art fair, Rosabella; Valeria was not fairer!"—

He bowed himself down to her, and imprinted a burning kiss on the pale cheeks of the beauty.

—" Leave me, thou dreadful man!" she stammered in terror; " oh! leave me!"—

—" Ah! Rosabella, why art thou so beauteous, and why am I.... Know'st thou who kist thy cheek, Rosabella? Go!

Go! tell thy uncle, the proud Doge, *'Twas the Bravo Abellino."—*

He said, and rushed out of the arbour.

CHAP. VII.

The Bravo's Bride.

It was not without good reason, that Abellino took his departure in such haste. He had quitted the spot but a few minutes, when a large party accidentally strolled that way, and discovered with astonishment the corse of Matteo, and Rosabella pale and trembling in the arbour.

A crowd immediately collected itself round

round them. It increased with every moment, and Rosabella was necessitated to repeat what had happened to her for the satisfaction of every new-comer.

In the mean while some of the Doge's courtiers, who happened to be among the crowd, hastened to call her attendants together; her gondola was already waiting for her, and the terrified girl soon reached her uncle's palace in safety.

In vain was an embargo laid upon every other gondola; in vain did they examine every person, who was in the Gardens of Dolabella at the time, when the murdered assassin was first discovered—No traces could be found of Abellino.

The

The report of this strange adventure spread like wild-fire through Venice.—Abellino [for Rosabella had preserved but too well in her memory that dreadful name, and by the relation of her danger had given it universal publicity] Abellino was the object of general wonder and curiosity. Every one pitied the poor Rosabella for what she had suffered, execrated the villain who had bribed Matteo to murder her, and endeavoured to connect the different circumstances together by the help of one hypothesis or other, among which it would have been difficult to decide which was the most improbable.

Every one, who heard the adventure, told it again, and every one who told it, added something of his own; till at length

length it was made into a compleat romantic novel, which might have been entitled with great propriety " The Power of Beauty:" for the Venetian gentlemen and ladies had settled the point among themselves completely to their own satisfaction, that Abellino would undoubtedly have assassinated Rosabella, had he not been prevented by her uncommon beauty. But though Abellino's interference had preserved her life, it was doubted much, whether this adventure would be at all relished by her destined bridegroom, the Prince of Monaldeschi, a Neapolitan of the first rank, possest of immense wealth and extensive influence. The Doge had for some time been secretly engaged in negociating a match between his niece and this powerful nobleman, who was soon expected to make

make his appearance at Venice. The motive of his journey, in spite of all the Doge's precautions, had been divulged, and it was no longer a secret to any but Rosabella, who had never seen the Prince, and could not imagine, why his expected visit should excite such general curiosity.

Thus far the story had been told much to Rosabella's credit; but at length the women began to envy her for her share in the adventure. The kiss, which she had received from the Bravo, afforded them an excellent opportunity for throwing out a few malicious insinuations—" She received a great service," said one, " and there's no saying how far the fair Rosabella in the warmth of gratitude may have been carried in rewarding

ing her preserver!"—" Very true," observed another, " and for my part I think it not very likely, that the fellow, being alone with a pretty girl whose life he had just saved, should have gone away contented with a single kiss!"— " Come, come," interrupted a third, " Do not let us judge uncharitably; the fact may be exactly as the lady relates it; though I *must* say, that gentlemen of Abellino's profession are not usually so pretty-behaved, and that this is the first time I ever heard of a Bravo in the Platonics."—

In short, Rosabella and the horrible Abellino furnished the indolent and gossiping Venetians with conversation so long, that at length the Doge's niece was universally known by the honourable

able appellation of " the Bravo's Bride."

But no one gave himself more trouble about this affair than the Doge, the good but proud Andreas. He immediately issued orders, that every person of suspicious appearance should be watched more closely than ever: the night-patroles were doubled; and spies were employed daily in procuring intelligence of Abellino: and yet was all in vain. Abellino's retreat was inscrutable.

CHAP. VIII.

The Conspiracy.

—" Confusion!" exclaimed Parozzi, a Venetian nobleman of the first rank, as he paced his chamber with a disordered air, on the morning after Matteo's murder; " now all curses light upon the villain's awkwardness! Yet it seems inconceivable to me, how all this should have fallen out so untowardly! Has any one discovered my designs?— I know well, that Verrino loves Rosabella;

bella; was it he, who opposed this confounded Abellino to Matteo, and charged him to mar my plans against her?—That seems likely—And now, when the Doge enquires who it was that employed assassins to murder his niece, what other will be suspected than Parozzi, the discontented lover to whom Rosabella refused her hand, and whom Andreas hates past hope of reconciliation?—And now having once found the scent.... Parozzi! Parozzi! should the crafty Andreas get an insight into your plans.... should he learn, that you have placed yourself at the head of a troop of hare-brained youths.... hare-brained may I well call children, who, in order to avoid the rod, set fire to their paternal mansion—Parozzi, should all this be revealed to Andreas....!"—

Here

Here his reflections were interrupted. Memmo, Falieri, and Contarino entered the room, three young Venetians of the highest rank, Parozzi's inseparable companions, men depraved both in mind and body, spendthrifts, voluptuaries, well known to every usurer in Venice, and owing more than their paternal inheritance would ever admit of their paying.

—" Why how is this, Parozzi?" cried Memmo as he entered, [a wretch whose every feature exhibited marks of that libertinism to which his life had been dedicated,] " I can scarce recover myself from my astonishment! For heaven's sake, is this report true? Did you really hire Matteo to murder the Doge's niece?"—

—" I?"

"I?" exclaimed Parozzi, and hastily turned away to hide the deadly paleness which overspread his countenance; "why should you suppose, that any such design.... surely Memmo, you are distracted."—

Memmo—By my soul, I speak but the plain matter of fact. Nay, only ask Falieri; he can tell you more.—

Falieri—Faith, it's certain, Parozzi, that Lomellino has declared to the Doge as a truth beyond doubting, that *you*, and none but *you*, were the person, who instigated Matteo to attempt Rosabella's life.

Parozzi—And I tell you again, that Lomellino knows not what he says.

Contarino

Contarino—Well, well! only be upon your guard. Andreas is a terrible fellow to deal with.

Falieri—*He* terrible? I tell you, he is the most contemptible blockhead that the universe can furnish! Courage perhaps he possesses, but of brains not an atom.

Contarino—And *I* tell you, that Andreas is as brave as a lion, and as crafty as a fox.

Falieri—Psha! psha! Every thing would go to the rack and ruin, were it not for the wiser heads of his triumvirate of counsellors, whom Heaven confound! Deprive him of Paolo Manfrone, Conari, and Lomellino, and the Doge would stand

stand there looking as foolish as a school-boy, who was going to be examined, and had forgotten his lesson.

Parozzi—Falieri is in the right.

Memmo—Quite! quite!

Falieri—And then Andreas is as proud as a beggar grown rich and drest in his first suit of embroidery! By St. Anthony, he is become quite insupportable!—Do you not observe how he increases the number of his attendants daily?

Memmo—Nay, that is an undoubted fact.

Contarino—And then to what an unbounded

bounded extent has he carried his influence!—the Signoria, the Quaranti, the Procurators of St. Mark, the Avocatori, all think, and act, exactly as it suits the Doge's pleasure and convenience! Every soul of them depends as much on that one man's humour and caprices, as puppets do, who nod or shake their wooden heads, just as the fellow behind the curtain thinks proper to move the wires.

Parozzi—And yet the populace idolizes this Andreas!

Memmo—Aye, that is the worst part of the story.

Falieri—But never credit me again, if he does not experience a reverse of fortune speedily.

Contarino

Contarino—That might happen, would we but set our shoulders to the wheel stoutly. But what do we do? We pass our time in taverns and brothels, drink, and game, and throw ourselves headlong into such an ocean of debts, that the best swimmer must sink at last. Let us resolve to make the attempt: let us seek recruits on all sides; let us labour with all our might and main: things must change; or if they do not, take my word for it, my friends, this world is no longer a world for us.

Memmo—Nay, it's a melancholy truth, that during the last half year my creditors have been ready to beat my door down with knocking; I am awakened out of my sleep in the morning, and lulled to rest again at night with no other music than their eternal clamours.

Parozzi—Ha! ha! ha!—As for me, I need not tell you how *I* am situated!

Falieri—Had we been less extravagant, we might at this moment have been sitting quietly in our palaces, and .... But as things stand now....

Parozzi—Well!—" as things stand now".... I verily believe, that Falieri is going to moralize!

Contarino—That is ever the way with old sinners, when they have lost the power to sin any longer: then they are ready enough to weep over their past life, and talk loudly about repentance and

and reformation. Now, for my own part, I am perfectly well satisfied with my wanderings from the common beaten paths of morality and prudence. They serve to convince me, that I am not one of your every-day men, who sit cramped up in the chimney-corner, lifeless and phlegmatic, and shudder, when they hear of any extraordinary occurrence. Nature evidently intended me to be a libertine, and I am determined to fulfil my destination.—Why, if spirits like ours were not produced every now and then, the world would absolutely go fast asleep: but we rouze it by deranging the old order of things, force mankind to quicken their snail's pace, furnish a million of idlers with riddles which they puzzle their brains about without being able to comprehend, infuse some few hundreds of new ideas into the heads of the great multitude, and, in short, are as useful to the world, as tempests are, which dissipate those exhalations, with which Nature otherwise would poison herself.

Falieri—Excellent sophistry, by my honour! Why, Contarino, antient Rome has had an irreparable loss in not having numbered you among her orators: it is a pity though, that there should be so little that's solid wrapt up in so many fine-sounding words.—Now learn, that while you, with this rare talent of eloquence, have been most unmercifully wearing out the patience of your good-natured hearers, Falieri has been in *action!* The Cardinal Gonzaga is discontented with the government; Heaven knows what

Andreas

Andreas has done to make him so vehemently his enemy; but, in short, Gonzaga now belongs to our party.

Parozzi—[with astonishment and delight]—Falieri, are you in your senses? —The Cardinal Gonzaga?

Falieri—Is ours, and ours both body and soul. I confess, I was first obliged to rhodomontade a good deal to him about our patriotism, our glorious designs, our love for freedom, and so forth; in short, Gonzaga is an hypocrite, and therefore is Gonzaga the fitter for us.

Contarino—[clasping Falieri's hand] —Bravo, my friend! Venice shall see a second edition of Catiline's conspiracy.—
Now

Now then it is *my* turn to speak, for I have not been idle since we parted. In truth I have as yet *caught* nothing, but I have made myself master of an all-powerful net, with which I doubt not to capture the best half of Venice. You all know the Marchioness Olympia?

Parozzi—Does not each of us keep a list of the handsomest women in the republic, and can we have forgotten number one?

Falieri—Olympia and Rosabella are the goddesses of Venice: our youths burn incense on no other altar.

Contarino—Olympia is my own.

Falieri—How?

Parozzi

Parozzi—Olympia?

Contarino—Why how now? Why stare ye, as had I prophecied to you that the skies were going to fall?—I tell you Olympia's heart is mine, and that I possess her entire and most intimate confidence. Our connection must remain a profound secret; but depend on it, whatever *I* wish, *she* wishes also, and you know she can make half the nobility in Venice dance to the sound of her pipe, let her play what tune she pleases.

Parozzi—Contarino, you are our master.

Contarino—And you had not the least suspicion, how powerful an ally I was labouring to procure for you?

Parozzi

Parozzi—I must blush for myself while I listen to you, since as yet I have done nothing. Yet this I must say in my excuse: had Matteo, bribed by my gold, accomplished Rosabella's murder, the Doge would have been robbed of that chain, with which he holds the chief men in Venice attached to his government. Andreas would have no merit, were Rosabella once removed. The most illustrious families would care no longer for his friendship, were their hopes of a connection with him by means of his niece buried in her grave. Rosabella will one day be the Doge's heiress.

Memmo—All that I can do for you in this business is to provide you with pecuniary supplies. My old miserable uncle, whose whole property becomes mine

at

at his death, has brim-full coffers, and the old miser dies whenever I say the word.

Falieri—You have suffered him to live too long already.

Memmo—Why, I never have been able to make up my mind entirely to... .. You would scarcely believe it, friends, but at times I am so hypochondriac, that I could almost fancy I feel twinges of conscience.

Contarino—Indeed! Then take my advice; go into a monastery.

Memmo—Yes, truly, that would suit me to an hair!

Falieri

Falieri—Our first care must be to find out our old acquaintances, Matteo's companions: yet having hitherto always transacted business with them through their Captain, I know not where they are to be met with.

Parozzi—As soon as they are found, their first employment must be the removal of the Doge's trio of advisers.

Contarino—That were an excellent idea, if it were but as easily done as said.——Well then, my friends, this principal point at least is decided. Either we will bury our debts under the ruins of the existing constitution of the republic, or make Andreas a gift of our heads towards strengthening the walls of the building—In either case we shall at least

least obtain quiet. Necessity with her whip of serpents has driven us to the very highest point of her rock, whence we must save ourselves by some act of extraordinary daring, or be precipitated on the opposite side into the abyss of shame and eternal oblivion. The next point to be considered is, how we may best obtain supplies for our necessary expenses, and induce others to join with us in our plans. For this purpose, we must use every artifice to secure in our interests the courtezans of the greatest celebrity in Venice. What *we* should be unable to effect by every power of persuasion, banditti by their daggers, and princes by their treasuries, can one of those Phrynes accomplish with a single look. Where the terrors of the scaffold are without effect, and the priest's ex-
hortations

hortations are heard with coldness, a wanton kiss and a tender promise often perform wonders. The most vigilant fidelity drops to sleep on the voluptuous bosoms of these witches; the warmth of their kisses can thaw the lips of Secrecy itself; and the bell which sounded the hour of assignation, has often rang the knell of the most sacred principles and most steadfast resolutions.—But should you either fail to gain the mastery over the minds of these women, or fear to be yourselves entangled in the nets which you wish to spread for others, in these cases you must have recourse to the holy father-confessors. Flatter the pride of these insolent Friars; paint for them upon the blank leaf of futurity bishop's mitres, patriarchal missions, the hats of cardinals, and the keys of St. Peter; my

My life upon it, they will spring at the bait, and you will have them completely, at your disposal. These hypocrites who govern the consciences of the bigotted Venetians, hold man and woman, the noble and the mendicant, the Doge and the gondoleer, bound fast in the chains of superstition, by which they can lead them wheresoever it best suits their pleasure—It will save us tons of gold in gaining over proselytes and keeping their consciences quiet when gained, if we can but obtain the assistance of the confessors, whose blessings and curses pass with the multitude for current coin.—Now then to work, comrades, and so farewell."—

CHAP. IX.

Cinthia's dwelling.

Scarcely had Abellino atchieved the bloody deed, which employed every tongue in Venice, than he changed his dress and whole appearance with so much expedition and success as to prevent the slightest suspicion of his being Matteo's murderer. He quitted the gardens unquestioned, nor left the least trace which could lead to a discovery.

He

He arrived at Cinthia's dwelling. It was already evening. Cinthia opened the door, and Abellino entered the common apartment.

—" Where are the rest?" said he in a savage tone of voice, whose sound made Cinthia tremble.

—" They have been asleep," she answered, " since mid-day. Probably they mean to go out on some pursuit to-night."—

Abellino threw himself into a chair, and seemed to be lost in thought.

—" But why are you always so gloomy, Abellino," said Cinthia, drawing near him; " it's that which makes you so ugly. Pry'thee away with those frowns; they make your countenance look worse than Nature made it."—

Abellino made no answer.

—" Really you are enough to frighten a body! Come now, let us be friends, Abellino: I begin not to dislike you, and to endure your appearance ; and I don't know but...."—

—" Go! wake the sleepers!" roared the Bravo.

—" The sleepers? Psha! let them sleep on, the stupid rogues! Sure you are not afraid to be alone with me? Mercy on me, one would think I looked as terrible as yourself? Do I?—Nay, look on me, Abellino!"—

Cinthia, to say the truth, was by no means an ill-looking girl; her eyes were bright and expressive; her hair fell in shining ringlets over her bosom; her lips were red and full, and she bowed them towards Abellino's—But Abellino's were still sacred by the touch of Rosabella's cheek—He started from his seat, and removed [yet gently] Cinthia's hand, which rested on his shoulder.

—" Wake the sleepers, my good girl," said he, " I must speak with them this moment."—

Cinthia hesitated.

—" Nay, go!" said he in a fierce voice.

Cinthia retired in silence; yet as she crost the threshold, she stopped for an instant, and menaced him with her finger.

Abellino strode through the chamber with hasty steps, his head reclining on his shoulder, his arms folded over his breast.

—" The first step is taken," said he to himself; " there is one moral monster the less on earth. I have committed no sin by this murder; I have but performed a sacred duty—Aid me, thou Great and Good, for arduous is the task before me.—Ah! should that task be gone

gone through with success, and Rosabella be the reward of my labours.... Rosabella?—What! shall the Doge's niece bestow on the outcast Abellino .... Oh! madman that I am to hope it, never can I reach the goal of my wishes! —No! never was there frenzy to equal mine! To attach myself at first sight to.... Yet Rosabella alone is capable of thus enchanting at first sight!—Rosabella and Valeria!—To be beloved by two such women...... Yet though 'tis impossible to attain, the *striving* to attain such an end is glorious! Illusions so delightful will at least make me happy for a moment, and alas! the wretched Abellino needs so much illusions, that for a moment will make him happy!— Oh! surely knew the world what I gladly *would* accomplish, the world would both love and pity me!"—

Cinthia returned—the four Bravos followed her, yawning, grumbling, and still half asleep.

—" Come, come!" said Abellino; " rouze yourselves, lads! Before I say anything, be convinced that you are wide awake, for what I am going to tell you is so strange, that you would scarce believe it in a dream."—

They listened to him with an air of indifference and impatience.

—" Why, what's the matter now?" said Thomaso, while he stretched himself.

—" Neither

—" Neither more nor less, than that our honest, hearty, brave Matteo.... is murdered!"

—" What!——Murdered?"—every one exclaimed, and gazed with looks of terror on the bearer of this unwelcome news; while Cinthia gave a loud scream, and clasping her hands together, sank almost breathless into a chair.—

A general silence prevailed for some time.

—" Murdered?" at length repeated Thomaso—" and by whom?"

Baluzzo—Where?

Pietrino—What? this forenoon?
                              Abellino

Abellino—In the gardens of Dolabella, where he was found bleeding at the feet of the Doge's niece.—Whether he fell by *her* hand, or by that of one of her admirers, I cannot say.

Cinthia—[weeping]—Poor dear Matteo!

Abellino—About this time to-morrow you will see his corse exhibited on the gibbet.

Pietrino—What! Did any one recognize him?

Abellino—Yes, yes! there's no doubt about his trade, you may depend on't.

Cinthia

Cinthia—The gibbet!—Poor dear Matteo!

Thomaso—This is a fine piece of work!

Baluzzo—Confound the fellow! who would have thought of any thing happening so unlucky!

Abellino—Why how now? You seem to be quite overcome?

Struzza—I cannot recover myself: surprize and terror have almost stupified me!

Abellino—Indeed! By my life, when I heard the news I burst into laughter—
' Signor

' Signor Matteo,' said I, ' I wish your worship joy of your safe arrival.'—

Thomaso—What?

Struzza—You laughed? Hang me if I can see what there is to laugh at!

Abellino—Why surely you are not afraid of receiving what you are so ready to bestow on others? What is your object? What can we expect as our reward at the end of our labours, except the gibbet or the rack? What memorials of our actions shall we leave behind us, except our skeletons dancing in the air, and the chains which rattle round them? He who chuses to play the Bravo's part on the great theatre of the world,

world, must not be afraid of death, whether it come at the hands of the physician or of the executioner.—Come, come! pluck up your spirits, comrades.

Thomaso—That's easy to say, but quite out of my power.

Pietrino—Mercy on me, how my teeth chatter!

Baluzzo—Pry'thee, Abellino, be composed for a moment or two! your gaiety at a time like this is quite horrible.

Cinthia—Oh! me! oh me!—Poor murdered Matteo!

Abellino—Hey-day! Why, what is all this?—Cinthia, my life, are you not
ashamed

ashamed of being such a child? Come, let you and I renew that conversation which my sending you to wake these gentlemen interrupted—Sit down by me, sweetheart, and give me a kiss.

Cinthia—Out upon you, monster!

Abellino—What, have you altered your mind, my pretty dear?—Well, well; with all my heart! When *you* are in the humour, perhaps *I* may not have the inclination.

Baluzzo—Death and the devil, Abellino, is this a time for talking nonsense? Pry'thee keep such trash for a fitter occasion, and let us consider what we are to do just now.

Pietrino

Pietrino—Nay, this is no season for trifling.

Struzza—Tell us, Abellino; you are a clever fellow; what course is it best for us to take?

Abellino—[after a pause]—Nothing, or a great deal—One of two things we must do—Either we must remain *where* we are, and *what* we are, murder honest men to please any rascal who will give us gold and fair words, and make up our minds to be hung, broken on the wheel, condemned to the gallows, burnt alive, crucified, or beheaded, at the long run, just as it may seem best to the supreme authority; or else....

Thomaso—Or else?—Well?
                                                Abellino

Abellino—Or else we must divide the spoils which are already in our possession, quit the republic, begin a new and better life, and endeavour to make our peace with Heaven.—We have already wealth enough to make it unnecessary for us to ask—" How shall we get our bread?"—You may either buy an estate in some foreign country, or keep an *Osteria*, or engage in commerce, or set up some trade, or, in short, do whatever you like best, so that you do but abandon the profession of an assassin. Then we may look out for a wife among the pretty girls of our own rank in life, become the happy fathers of sons and daughters, may eat and drink in peace and security, and make amends by the honesty of our future lives for the offences of our past.

Thomaso

Thomaso—Ha! ha! ha!

Abellino—What *you* do, that will *I* do too; I will either hang or be broken on the wheel along with you, or become an honest man, just as you please—Now then, what is your decision?

Thomaso—Was there ever such a stupid counsellor!

Pietrino—Our decision?—Nay, the point's not very difficult to decide.

Abellino—I should have thought it *had* been.

Thomaso—Without more words then, I vote for our remaining as we are, and carrying on our old trade: that will bring us in plenty of gold, and enable us to lead a jolly life.

Pietrino—Right, lad! You speak my thoughts exactly.

Thomaso—We are Bravos, it's true; but what then? We are honest fellows, and the devil take him who dares to say we are not. However, at any rate we must keep within doors for a few days, lest we should be discovered; for I warrant you the Doge's spies are abroad in search of us by this. But as soon as the pursuit is over, be it our first business to find out Matteo's murderer, and throttle him out of hand as a warning to all others.

All—Bravo! bravissimo!

Pietrino

Pietrino—And from this day forth I vote, that Thomaso should be our Captain.

Struzza—Aye, in Matteo's stead.

All—Right! right!

Abellino—To which I say amen with all my heart—Now then all is decided.

End of Book the First.

BOOK THE SECOND.

CHAP. I.

The Birth-day.

In solitude and anxiety, with barred windows and bolted doors, did the banditti pass the day immediately succeeding Matteo's murder; every murmur in the street appeared to them a cause of apprehension; every foot-step which approached their doors made them tremble till it had passed them.

In the mean while the ducal palace blazed. with splendour and resounded with mirth. The Doge celebrated the birth-day of his fair niece, Rosabella; and the feast was honoured by the presence of the chief persons of the city, of the foreign ambassadors, and of many illustrious strangers who were at that time resident in Venice.

On this occasion no expense had been spared, no source of pleasure had been neglected. The arts contended with each other for superiority; the best poets in Venice celebrated this day with powers excelling any thing which they had before exhibited, for the subject of their verses was Rosabella: the musicians and *virtuosi* surpassed all their former triumphs, for their object was to obtain

the

the suffrage of Rosabella. The singular union of all kinds of pleasure intoxicated the imagination of every guest; and the Genius of Delight extended his influence over the whole assembly, over the old man and the youth, over the matron and the virgin.

The venerable Andreas had seldom been seen in such high spirits, as on this occasion.—He was all life; smiles of satisfaction played round his lips; gracious and condescending to every one, he made it his chief care to prevent his rank from being felt. Sometimes he trifled with the ladies, whose beauty formed the greatest ornament of this entertainment; sometimes he mingled among the masks, whose fantastic appearance and gaiety of conversation enlivened

livened the ball-room by their variety; at other times he played chess with the generals and admirals of the republic; and frequently he forsook every thing to gaze with delight on Rosabella's dancing, or listen in silent rapture to Rosabella's music.

Lomellino, Conari, and Paolo Manfrone, the Doge's three confidential friends and counsellors, in defiance of their grey hairs, mingled in the throng of youthful beauties, flirted first with one, and then with another, and the arrows of raillery were darted and received on both sides with spirit and good humour.

—" Now, Lomellino," said Andreas to his friend, who entered the saloon, in which the Doge was at that time accidentally alone with his niece; " you seem in gayer spirits this evening than when we were lying before Scardona, and had so hard a game to play against the Turks."—

Lomellino—I shall not take upon me to deny that, Signor. I still think with mixture of terror and satisfaction on the night when we took Scardona, and carried the half-moon before the city walls. By my soul, our Venetians fought like lions.

Andreas—Fill this goblet to their memory, my old soldier; you have earned your rest bravely.

Lomellino—Aye, Signor, and oh! it is

is so sweet to rest on laurels!—But in truth, 'tis to *you* that I am indebted for mine—it is you who have immortalized me. No soul on earth would have known that Lomellino existed, had he not fought in Dalmatia and Sicilia under the banners of the great Andreas, and assisted him in raising eternal trophies in honour of the republic.

Andreas—My good Lomellino, the Cyprus wine has heated your imagination.

Lomellino—Nay, I know well I ought not to call you great, and praise you thus openly to your face; but faith! Signor, I am grown too old for it to be worth my while to flatter. That is a business which I leave to our young courtiers, who have never yet come within the smell of powder, and never have fought for Venice and Andreas.

Andreas—You are an old enthusiast! —Think you the Emperor is of the same opinion?

Lomellino—Unless Charles the Fifth is deceived by those about him, or is too proud to allow the greatness of an enemy, he must say perforce—" There is but one man on earth whom I fear, and who is worthy to contend with me; and that man is Andreas."—

Andreas—I suspect he will be sorely displeased when he receives my answer to the message by which he notified to

me

me the imprisonment of the French King.

Lomellino—Displeased he will be, Signor, no doubt of it: but what then? Venice need not fear his displeasure, while Andreas still lives. But when you and your heroes are once gone to your eternal rest. . . . then alas for thee, poor Venice! I fear your golden times will soon come to their conclusion.

Andreas—What? Have we not many young officers of great promise?

Lomellino—Alas! what are most of them? Heroes in the fields of Venus! Heroes at a drinking-bout! Effeminate striplings, relaxed both in mind and body!—But how I am running on, for-
getful

getful. . . . Ah! when one is grown old, and conversing with an Andreas, it is easy to forget every thing else—My Lord, I sought you with a request; a request too of consequence.

Andreas—You excite my curiosity.

Lomellino—About a week ago, there arrived here a young Florentine nobleman called Flodoardo, a youth of noble appearance and great promise.

Andreas—Well?

Lomellino—His father was one of my dearest friends; he is dead now, the good old generous nobleman! In our youth we served together on board the same vessel, and many a turbaned head has

has fallen beneath his sword—Ah! he was a brave soldier.

Andreas—While celebrating the father's bravery, you seem to have quite forgotten the son.

Lomellino—His son is arrived in Venice, and wishes to enter into the service of the republic. I intreat you, give the young man some respectable situation; he will prove the boast of Venice, when we shall be in our graves; on that would I hazard my existence!

Andreas—Has he sense and talent?

Lomellino—That he has, and an heart like his father's—Will it please you to see and converse with him? He is yonder,

der, among the masks in the great Saloon. One thing I must tell you, as a specimen of his designs. He has heard of the banditti who infest Venice; and he engages, that the first piece of service which he renders the republic shall be the delivering into the hands of justice these concealed assassins, who hitherto have eluded the vigilance of our police.

Andreas—Indeed?—I doubt that promise will be too much for his power to perform—Flodoardo, I think you called him?—Tell him I would speak with him.

Lomellino—Oh! then I have gained at least the *half* of my cause, and I believe the *whole* of it; for to see Flodoardo, and not to like him, is as difficult

as

as to look at Paradise and not wish to enter. To see Flodoardo, and to hate him, is as unlikely, as that a blind man should hate the kind hand which removes the cataract from his eyes, and pours upon them the blessings of light and beauties of Nature.

Andreas—[smiling]—In the whole course of our acquaintance, Lomellino, never did I hear you so enthusiastic!— Go then; conduct this prodigy hither.

Lomellino—I hasten to find him— And as for you, Signora, look to yourself! look to yourself, I say!

Rosabella—Nay, pry'thee, Lomellino, bring your hero hither without delay;
you

you have raised my curiosity to the height.

Lomellino quitted the Saloon.

Andreas—How comes it that you rejoin not the dancers, my child?

Rosabella—I am weary, and besides curiosity now detains me here, for I would fain see this Flodoardo, whom Lomellino thinks deserving of such extraordinary praise. Shall I tell you the truth, my dear uncle? I verily believe that I am already acquainted with him. There was a mask in a Grecian habit, whose appearance was so striking, that it was impossible for him to remain confounded with the crowd: the least attentive

tentive eye must have singled him out from among a thousand. It was a tall light figure, so graceful in every movement.... then his dancing was quite perfection.

Andreas—[smiling, and threatening with his finger]—Child! child!

Rosabella—Nay, my dear uncle, what I say is mere justice: it is possible, indeed, that the Greek and the Florentine may be two different persons; but still, according to Lomellino's description.... Oh! look, dear uncle, only look yonder! there stands the Greek, as I live.

Andreas—And Lomellino is with him —they approach—Rosabella, you have made a good guess.

The

The Doge had scarcely ceased to speak, when Lomellino entered the room, conducting a tall young man, richly habited in the Grecian fashion.

—" My gracious Lord," said Lomellino, " I present to you the Count Flodoardo, who humbly sues for your protection."

Flodoardo uncovered his head in token of respect, took off his mask, and bowed low before the illustrious ruler of Venice.

Andreas—I understand you are desirous of serving the republic ?

Flodoardo—That is my ambition,
should

should your Highness think me deserving of such an honour.

Andreas—Lomellino speaks highly of you; if all that he says be true, how came you to deprive your own country of your services?

Flodoardo—Because my own country is not governed by an Andreas.

Andreas—You have intentions, it seems, of discovering the haunts of the banditti, who for some time past have caused so many tears to flow in Venice?

Flodoardo—If your Highness would deign to confide in me, I would answer with my head for their delivery into the hands of your officers, and that speedily.

Andreas—That were much for a stranger to perform—I would fain make the trial whether you can keep your word.

Flodoardo—That is sufficient—To-morrow, or the day after at latest, will I perform my promise.

Andreas—And you make that promise so resolutely? Are you aware, young man, how dangerous a task it is to surprize these miscreants? They are never to be found when sought for, and always present when least expected; they are at once every where, and no where; there exists not a nook in all Venice which

which our spies are not acquainted with, or have left unexamined, and yet has our police endeavoured in vain to discover the place of their concealment.

Flodoardo—I know all this, and to know it rejoices me, since it affords me an opportunity of convincing the Doge of Venice, that my actions are not those of a common adventurer.

Andreas—Perform your promise, and then let me hear of you. For the present our discourse shall end here, for no unpleasant thoughts must disturb the joy to which this day is dedicated.—Rosabella, would you not like to join the dancers?—Count, I confide her to your care.

Flodoardo—I could not be intrusted with a more precious charge.

Rosabella, during this conversation, had been leaning against the back of her uncle's chair: she repeated to herself Lomellino's assertion, " that to see Flodoardo, and not to like him, was as difficult as to look at Paradise and not wish to enter ;" and while she gazed on the youth, she allowed that Lomellino had not exaggerated. When her uncle desired Flodoardo to conduct her to the dancers, a soft blush overspread her cheeks, and she doubted whether she should accept or decline the hand which was immediately offered.

And to tell you my real opinion, my fair Ladies, I suspect that very few of you

you would have been more collected than Rosabella, had you found yourselves similarly situated. In truth, such a form as Flodoardo's; a countenance whose physiognomy seemed a passport at once to the hearts of all who examined it; features so exquisitely fashioned, that the artist who wished to execute a model of manly beauty, had he imitated them, would have had nothing to supply or improve; features, every one of which spoke so clearly—" the bosom of this youth contains the heart of an hero"—...... Ah! Ladies, my dear Ladies, a man like this might well make some little confusion in the head and heart of a poor young girl, tender, and unsuspicious!

Flodoardo took Rosabella's hand, and led

led her into the ball-room. Here all was mirth and splendour; the roofs re-echoed with the full swell of harmony, and the floor trembled beneath the multitude of dancers, who formed a thousand beautiful groupes by the blaze of innumerable lustres—Yet Flodoardo and Rosabella past on in silence, till they reached the extreme end of the Great Saloon. Here they stopped, and remained before an open window. Some minutes past, and still they spoke not.—Sometimes they gazed on each other; sometimes on the dancers, sometimes on the moon; and then again they forgot each other, the dancers, and the moon, and were totally absorbed in themselves.

—" Lady," said Flodoardo at length, " can there be a greater misfortune!"
—" A mis-

—" A misfortune?" said Rosabella, starting, as if suddenly awaking from a dream ; " what misfortune, Signor? who is unfortunate?"—

—" He who is doomed to behold the joys of Elysium, and never to possess them ; he who dies of thirst, and sees a cup stand full before him, but which he knows is destined for the lips of another!"—

—" And are you, my Lord, this outcast from Elysium? are you the thirsty one who stands near the cup which is filled for another? Is it thus that you wish me to understand your speech?"—

—" You understand it as I meant ; and

and now tell me, lovely Rosabella, am I not indeed unfortunate?"—

—" And where then is the Elysium which you never must possess?"—

—" Where Rosabella is, there is Elysium."—

Rosabella blushed, and cast her eyes on the ground.

—" You are not offended, Signora ?" said Flodoardo, and took her hand with an air of respectful tenderness; " has this openness displeased you ?"—

—" You are a native of Florence, Count Flodoardo? In Venice we dislike

like these kind of compliments; at least *I* dislike them, and wish to hear them from no one less than from you."—

—" By my life, Signora, I spoke but as I thought; my words concealed no flattery."—

—" See! the Doge enters the saloon with Manfrone and Lomellino; he will seek us among the dancers. Come, let us join them."—

Flodoardo followed her in silence. The dance began. Heavens! how lovely looked Rosabella as she glided along to the sweet sounds of music, conducted by Flodoardo! How handsome looked Flodoardo, as lighter than air he flew down the dance, while his brilliant eyes saw no object but Rosabella! He was still without his mask, and bare-headed; but every eye glanced away from the helmets and *barrettes*, waving with plumes and sparkling with jewels, to gaze on Flodoardo's raven locks, as they floated on the air in wild luxuriance. A murmur of admiration rose from every corner of the saloon, but it rose unmarked by those who were the objects of it: neither Rosabella nor Flodoardo at that moment formed a wish to be applauded, except by each other.

CHAP. II.

The Florentine Stranger.

Two evenings had elapsed since the Doge's entertainment; on the second Parozzi sat in his own apartment with Memmo and Falieri. Dimly burnt the lights; lowering and tempestuous were the skies without; gloomy and fearful were the souls of the libertines within.

Parozzi—[after a long silence]—What? are you both dreaming? Ho there!

there! Memmo, Falieri, fill your goblets.

Memmo—[with indifference]—Well! to please you.... —But I care not for wine to-night.

Falieri—Nor I.—Methinks it tastes like vinegar—Yet the wine itself is good; 'tis our ill-temper spoils it.

Parozzi—Confound the rascals!

Memmo—What? the banditti?

Parozzi—Not a trace of them can be found! It is enough to kill one with vexation!

Falieri—And in the mean while the time

time runs out, our projects will get wind, and then we shall sit quietly in the state prisons of Venice, objects of derision to the populace and ourselves! I could tear my flesh for anger!—[An universal silence.]

Parozzi—[striking his hand against the table passionately]—Flodoardo! Flodoardo!

Falieri—In a couple of hours I must attend the Cardinal Gonzaga! and what intelligence shall I have to give him?

Memmo—Come, come! Contarino cannot have been absent so long without cause; I warrant you, he will bring some news with him when he arrives.

Falieri

Falieri—Psha! psha! My life on't, he lies at this moment at Olympia's feet, and forgets us, the republic, the banditti, and himself.

Parozzi—And so neither of you know any thing of this Flodoardo?

Memmo—No more than of what happened on Rosabella's birth-day.

Falieri—Well then, I know *one* thing more about him; Parozzi is jealous of him.

Parozzi—I? Ridiculous! Rosabella may bestow her hand on the German Emperor, or a Venetian Gondoleer, without its giving *me* the least anxiety.

Falieri

Falieri—Ha! ha! ha!

Memmo—Well, one thing at least even Envy must confess; Flodoardo is the handsomest man in Venice. I doubt whether there's a woman in the city who has virtue enough to resist him.

Parozzi—And *I* should doubt it too, if women had as little sense as *you* have, and looked only at the shell, without minding the kernel....

Memmo—Which unluckily is exactly the thing which women always do.

Falieri—The old Lomellino seems to be extremely intimate with this Flodoardo; they say he was well acquainted with his father.

Memmo—It was he who presented him to the Doge.

Parozzi—Hark!—Surely some one knocked at the palace-door?

Memmo—It can be none but Contarino. Now then we shall hear whether he has discovered the banditti.

Falieri—[starting from his chair]—I'll swear to that footstep! it's Contarino!

The doors were thrown open: Contarino entered hastily, enveloped in his cloak.

—" Good evening, sweet gentlemen!" said he, and threw his mantle aside.—
And

And Memmo, Parozzi, and Falieri started back in horror.

—" Good God!" they exclaimed, " what has happened? You are covered with blood?"—

—" A trifle!" cried Contarino; " is that wine? quick! give me a goblet of it! I expire with thirst."—

Falieri—[while he gives him a cup]— But, Contarino! you bleed?

Contarino—You need not tell me that —I did not do it myself, I promise you—

Parozzi—First let us bind up your wounds, and then tell us what has happened

pened to you—It is as well that the servants should remain ignorant of your adventure; I will be your surgeon myself.

Contarino—What has happened to me, say you? Oh! a joke, gentlemen! a mere joke!—Here, Falieri, fill the bowl again.

Memmo—I can scarcely breathe for terror!

Contarino—Very possibly; neither should *I*, were I Memmo, instead of being Contarino—the wound bleeds plenteously it's true, but it's by no means dangerous—[He tore open his doublet, and uncovered his bosom]—There look, comrades!

comrades! you see it's only a cut of not more than two inches deep.

Memmo—[shuddering]—Mercy on me! the very sight of it makes my blood run cold.

Parozzi brought ointments and linen, and bound up the wound of his associate.

Contarino—Old Horace is in the right: a philosopher can be any thing he pleases, a cobler, a king, or a physician. Only observe with what dignified address the philosopher Parozzi spreads that plaister for me!—I thank you, friend; that's enough—And now, comrades, place yourselves in a circle round me, me, and listen to the wonders which I am going to relate.

Falieri—Proceed.

Contarino—As soon as it was twilight, I stole out, wrapped in my cloak, determined if possible to discover some of the banditti: I knew not their persons, neither were they acquainted with mine. An extravagant undertaking, perhaps you will tell me; but I was resolved to convince you, that every thing which a man *determines* to do, may be done. I had some information respecting the rascals, though it was but slight, and on these grounds I proceeded—I happened by mere accident to stumble upon a gondoleer, whose appearance excited

cited my curiosity. I fell into discourse with him; I soon was convinced that he was not ignorant of the lurking-place of the Bravos, and by means of some gold and many fair speeches, I at length brought him to confess, that though not regularly belonging to the band, he had occasionally been employed by them. I immediately made a bargain with him; he conducted me in his gondola through the greatest part of Venice, sometimes right, sometimes left, till at length I lost every idea as to the quarter of the town in which I found myself. At length he insisted on binding my eyes with his handkerchief, and I was compelled to submit to this condition.—Half an hour elapsed before the gondola stopped; he told me to descend, conducted me through a couple of streets, and at length knocked

knocked at a door, where he left me still blindfolded—the door was opened; my business was inquired with great caution, and after some demur I was at length admitted. The handkerchief was now withdrawn from my eyes, and I found myself in a small chamber, surrounded by four men of not the most creditable appearance, and a young woman, who [it seems] had opened the door for me.

Falieri—You are a daring fellow, Contarino!

Contarino—Here was no time to be lost. I instantly threw my purse on the table, promised them mountains of gold, and fixed on particular days, hours, and signals, which were necessary to facilitate our future intercourse. For the present

present I only required that Manfrone, Conari, and Lomellino should be removed with all possible expedition.

All—Bravo!

Contarino—So far every thing went exactly as we could have wished; and one of my new associates was just setting out to guide me home, when we were surprised by an unexpected visit.

Parozzi—Well?

Memmo—[anxiously]—Go on for God's sake!

Contarino—A knocking was heard at the door; the girl went to enquire the cause;

cause; in an instant she returned pale as a corse, and—" Fly! fly!" cried she.

Falieri—What followed?

Contarino—Why then followed a whole legion of sbirri, and police-officers, and who should be at their head but. . . . the Florentine stranger!

All—Flodoardo? what, Flodoardo?

Contarino—Flodoardo.

Falieri—What demon could have guided him thither!

Parozzi—Hell and furies! Oh! that *I* had been there!

Memmo

Memmo—There now, Parozzi! you see at least that Flodoardo is no coward.

Falieri—Hush! let us hear the rest.

Contarino—We stood, as if we had been petrified; not a soul could stir a finger.—" In the name of the Doge and the republic," cried Flodoardo, " yield yourselves, and deliver your arms."— " The devil shall yield himself sooner than we!" exclaimed one of the banditti, and forced a sword from one of the officers: the others snatched their musquets from the walls; and as for me, my first care was to extinguish the lamp, so that we could not tell friends from foes—But still the confounded moonshine gleamed through the window-shutters, and shed a partial light through the

the room.—" Look to yourself, Contarino!" thought I; " if you are found here, you will be hanged for company!" and I drew my sword, and made a lunge at Flodoardo—But, however well-intended, my thrust was foiled by his sabre, which he whirled around with the rapidity of lightning. I fought like a madman, but all my skill was without effect on this occasion, and before I was aware of it, Flodoardo ripped open my bosom. I felt myself wounded, and sprang back; at that moment two pistols were fired, and the flash discovered to me a small side-door, which they had neglected to beset; through this I stole unperceived into the adjoining chamber, burst open the grated window, sprang below unhurt, crost a court-yard, climbed two or three garden-walls, gained the canal,

canal, where a gondola fortunately was waiting, persuaded the boatman to convey me with all speed to the Place of St. Mark, and thence hastened hither, astonished to find myself still alive—There is an infernal adventure for you!

Parozzi—I shall go mad!

Falieri—Every thing we design is counteracted! the more trouble we give ourselves, the further are we from the goal!

Memmo—I confess it seems to me as if Heaven gave us warning to desist— How say you?

Contarino—Psha! these are trifles! —Such accidents should only serve to sharpen

sharpen our wits!—the more obstacles I encounter, the firmer is my resolution to surmount them.

Falieri—Do the banditti know who you are?

Contarino—No; they are not only ignorant of my name, but suppose me to be a mere instrument of some powerful man, who has been injured by the ducal confederates.

Memmo—Well, Contarino, in my mind you should thank Heaven that you have escaped so well!

Falieri—But since he is an absolute stranger in Venice, how could Flodoardo discover

discover the lurking-place of the banditti?

Contarino—I know not—Probably by mere accident, like myself.—But by the Power that made me, he shall pay dearly for this wound!

Falieri—Flodoardo is rather too hasty in making himself remarked.

Parozzi—Flodoardo must die!

Contarino—[filling a goblet]—May his next cup contain poison!

Falieri—I shall do myself the honour of becoming better acquainted with the gentleman.

Contarino

Contarino—Memmo, we must needs have full purses, or our business will hang on hand woefully—When does your uncle take his departure to a better world?

Memmo—To-morrow evening!—and yet.... Ugh! I tremble!

CHAP. III.

More confusion.

SINCE Rosabella's birth-day, no woman in Venice who had the slightest pretensions to beauty, or the most remote expectations of making conquests, had any subject of conversation except the handsome Florentine: he found employment for every female tongue, and she who dared not employ her tongue, made amends for the privation with her thoughts. Many a maiden now enjoyed less

less tranquil slumbers; many an experienced coquette sighed, as she laid on her colour at the looking-glass; many a prude forgot the rules which she had laid down, and daily frequented the gardens and public walks, in which report gave her the hope of meeting Flodoardo.

But from the time that, placing himself at the head of the sbirri, he had dared to enter boldly the den of the banditti, and seize them at the hazard of his life, he was scarcely more an object of attention among the women than among the men. Greatly did they admire his courage and unshaken presence of mind, while engaged in so dangerous an adventure; but still more were they astonished at his penetration in discovering

ing where the Bravos concealed themselves, an attempt which had foiled even the keen wits of the so much celebrated police of Venice.

The Doge Andrèas cultivated the acquaintance of this singular young man with increasing assiduity; and the more he conversed with him, the more deserving of consideration did Flodoardo appear. The action by which he had rendered the republic a service so essential, was rewarded by a present that would not have disgraced imperial gratitude; and one of the most important offices in the state was confided to his superintendance.

Both favours were conferred unsolicited; but no sooner was the Florentine

tine apprized of the Doge's benevolent care of him, than with modesty and respect he requested to decline the proposed advantages. The only favour which he requested was, to be permitted to live free and independent in Venice during a year; at the end of which he promised to name that employment which he esteemed the best adapted to his abilities and inclination.

Flodoardo was lodged in the magnificent palace of his good old patron Lomellino: here he lived in the closest retirement, studied the most valuable parts of antient and modern literature, remained for whole days together in his own apartment, and was seldom to be seen in public except upon some great solemnity.

But

But the Doge, Lomellino, Manfrone, and Conari, men, who had established the fame of Venice on so firm a basis that it would require centuries to undermine it; men, in whose society one seemed to be withdrawn from the circle of ordinary mortals, and honoured by the intercourse of superior beings; men, who now graciously received the Florentine stranger into their intimacy, and resolved to spare no pains in forming him to support the character of a great man; it could not long escape the observation of men like these, that Flodoardo's gaiety was assumed, and that a secret sorrow preyed upon his heart.

In vain did Lomellino, who loved him like a father, endeavour to discover the source of his melancholy; in vain did the venerable Doge exert himself to disperse the gloom which opprest his young favourite; Flodoardo remained silent and sad.

And Rosabella?——Rosabella would have belied her sex, had she remained gay while Flodoardo sorrowed. Her spirits were flown; her eyes were frequently obscured with tears. She grew daily paler and paler; till the Doge, who doated on her, was seriously alarmed for her health—at length Rosabella grew really ill; a fever fixed itself upon her; she became weak, and was confined to her chamber, and her complaint baffled the skill of the most experienced physicians in Venice.

In the midst of these unpleasant circumstances

cumstances in which Andreas and his friends now found themselves, an incident occurred one morning, which raised their uneasiness to the very highest pitch. Never had so bold and audacious an action been heard of in Venice, as that which I am now going to relate.

The four banditti, whom Flodoardo had seized, Pietrino, Struzza, Baluzzo, and Thomaso, had been safely committed to the Doge's dungeons, where they underwent a daily examination, and looked upon every sun that rose, as the last that would ever rise for *them*. Andreas and his confidential counsellors now flattered themselves that the public tranquillity had nothing more to apprehend, and that Venice was compleatly purified of the miscreants, whom gold could

could bribe to be the instruments of revenge and cruelty.... when all at once the following address was discovered, affixed to most of the remarkable statues, and pasted against the corners of the principal streets, and pillars of the public buildings.

VENETIANS!

Struzza, Thomaso, Pietrino, Baluzzo, and Matteo, five as brave men as the world ever produced; who, had they stood at the head of armies, would have been called *heroes*, and now being called *banditti*, are fallen victims to the injustice of state-policy; these men, it is true, exist for you no longer: but their place is supplied by him, whose name is affixed to this paper, and who will stand by his employers with body and with soul!

soul! I laugh at the vigilance of the Venetian police; I laugh at the crafty and insolent Florentine, whose hand has dragged my brethren to the rack! Let those who need me, seek me; they will find me every where! Let those who search for me with the design of delivering me up to the law, despair and tremble: they will find me no-where—But *I* shall find *them*, and that when they least expect me!—Venetians, you understand me!—Woe to the man who shall attempt to discover me; his life and death depend upon my pleasure.—This comes from the Venetian Bravo,

ABELLINO.

—" An

—" An hundred sequins," exclaimed the incensed Doge on reading the paper, " an hundred sequins to him who discovers this monster Abellino, and a thousand to him who delivers him up to justice!"—

But in vain did spies ransack every lurking-place in Venice; no Abellino was to be found. In vain did the luxurious, the avaricious, and the hungry stretch their wits to the utmost, incited by the tempting promise of a thousand sequins. Abellino's prudence set all their ingenuity at defiance.

But not the less did every one assert that he had recognized Abellino sometimes in one disguise, and sometimes in another; as an old man, a gondoleer, a woman,

woman, or a monk. Every body had seen him somewhere; but unluckily nobody could tell where he was to be seen again.

CHAP. IV.

The Violet.

I informed my readers, in the beginning of the last chapter, that Flodoardo was become melancholy, and that Rosabella was indisposed: but I did not tell them what had occasioned this sudden change.

Flodoardo, who on his first arrival at Venice was all gaiety, and the life of every society in which he mingled, lost his

his spirits on one particular day; and it so happened, that it was on the very same day that Rosabella betrayed the first symptoms of indisposition.

For on this unlucky day did the caprice of accident, or perhaps the Goddess of Love [who has her caprices too every now and then] conduct Rosabella into her uncle's garden, which none but the Doge's intimate friends were permitted to enter, and where the Doge himself frequently reposed himself in solitude and silence during the evening hours of a sultry day.

Rosabella, lost in thought, wandered listless and unconscious along the broad and shady alleys of the garden. Sometimes, in a moment of vexation, she

plucked

plucked the unoffending leaves from the hedges, and strewed them upon the ground; sometimes she stopped suddenly, then rushed forward with impetuosity, then again stood still, and gazed upon the clear blue heaven. Sometimes her beautiful bosom was heaved with quick and irregular motion: and sometimes an half-supprest sigh escaped from her lips of coral.

—" He is very handsome!" she murmured, and gazed with such eagerness on vacancy, as had she seen there something which was hidden from the sight of common observers.

—" Yet Camilla is in the right!" she resumed after a pause; and she frowned as had she said that Camilla was in the wrong.

This Camilla was her governess, her friend, her confidante, I may almost say her mother. Rosabella had lost her parents early: her mother died when her child could scarcely lisp her name; and her father, Guiscardo of Corfu, the commander of a Venetian vessel, eight years before had perished in an engagement with the Turks, while he was still in the prime of life. Camilla, one of the worthiest creatures that ever dignified the name of woman, supplied to Rosabella the place of mother, had brought her up from infancy, and was now her best friend, and the person to whose ear she confided all her little secrets.

While

While Rosabella was still buried in her own reflections, the excellent Camilla advanced from a side-path, and hastened to join her pupil. Rosabella started.

Rosabella—Ah! dear Camilla, is it you? What brings you hither?

Camilla—You often call me your guardian angel, and guardian angels should always be near the object of their care.

Rosabella—Camilla, I have been thinking over your arguments; I cannot deny that all you have said to me is very true, and very wise; but still....

Camilla—But still, though your prudence

dence agrees with me, your heart is of a contrary opinion?

Rosabella—It is indeed.

Camilla—Nor do I blame your heart for differing from me, my poor girl! I have acknowledged to you without disguise that were *I* at your time of life, and were such a man as Flodoardo to throw himself in my way, I could not receive his attentions with indifference. It cannot be denied, that this young stranger is an uncommonly pleasing, and indeed, for any woman whose heart is disengaged, an uncommonly *dangerous* companion.—There is something very prepossessing in his appearance; his manners are elegant, and short as has been his abode in Venice, it is already past doubting that there are many noble and striking features in his character—But alas! after all, he is but a poor nobleman, and it is not very probable that the rich and powerful Doge of Venice will ever bestow his niece on one, who, to speak plainly, arrived here little better than a beggar. No, no, child, believe me; a romantic adventurer is no fit husband for Rosabella of Corfu.

Rosabella—Dear Camilla, who was talking about husbands? What I feel for Flodoardo is merely affection, friendship......

Camilla—Indeed? Then you would be perfectly satisfied, should some one of our wealthy ladies bestow her hand on Flodoardo?

Rosabella

Rosabella—[hastily]—Oh! Flodoardo would not *accept* her hand, Camilla, of that I am sure.

Camilla—Child! child! you would willingly deceive yourself! But be assured, that a girl who loves ever connects [perhaps unconsciously] the wish for an eternal *union* with the idea of an eternal *affection*. Now this is a wish which you cannot indulge in regard to Flodoardo, without seriously offending your uncle, who, good man as he is, must still submit to the severe controul of politics and etiquette.

Rosabella—I know all that, Camilla; but can I not make you comprehend that I am not in love with Flodoardo. and do not mean to be in love with him, and that love has nothing at all to do in the business? I repeat to you, what I feel for him is nothing but sincere and fervent friendship, and surely Flodoardo deserves that I should feel that sentiment for him—Deserves it, said I? Oh! what does Flodoardo *not* deserve!

Camilla—Aye, aye! friendship indeed .... and love.... Oh! Rosabella, you know not how often these deceivers borrow each other's mask to ensnare the hearts of unsuspecting maidens! you know not how often love finds admission when wrapt in friendship's cloak, into that bosom, which, had he approached under his own appearance, would have been closed against him for ever!—In short, my child, reflect how much you owe to your uncle; reflect how much uneasiness

uneasiness this inclination would cost him; and sacrifice to duty what at present is a mere caprice, but which, if encouraged, might make too deep an impression on your heart to be afterwards removed by your best efforts.

Rosabella—You say right, Camilla; I really believe myself that my prepossession in Flodoardo's favour is merely an accidental fancy, of which I shall easily get the better. No, no; I am not in love with Flodoardo, of that you may rest assured; I even think, that I rather feel an antipathy towards him, since you have shown me the possibility of his making me prove a cause of uneasiness to my kind, my excellent uncle.

Camilla—[smiling]—Are your sentiments

ments of duty and gratitude so *very* strong?

Rosabella—Oh! that they are, Camilla, and so you will say yourself hereafter—This disagreeable Flodoardo.... to give me so much vexation!—I wish he had never come to Venice! I declare I do not like him at all!

Camilla—No?—What? Not like Flodoardo?

Rosabella—[casting down her eyes]— No; not at all—Not that I wish him ill either; for you know, Camilla, there's no reason why I should *hate* this poor Flodoardo?

Camilla—Well, we will resume this subject

subject when I return; I have business, and the gondola waits for me—Farewell, my child, and do not lay aside your resolution as hastily as you took it up!

Camilla departed; and Rosabella remained melancholy and uncertain; she built castles in the air, and destroyed them as soon as built; she formed wishes, and condemned herself for having formed them; she looked round her frequently in search of something, but dared not confess to herself what it was of which she was in search.

The evening was sultry, and Rosabella was compelled to shelter herself from the sun's overpowering heat. In the garden was a small fountain, bordered by a bank of moss, over which

the

the magic hands of art and nature had formed a canopy of ivy and jessamine. Thither she bent her steps; she arrived at the fountain.... and instantly drew back, covered with blushes—For on the bank of moss, shaded by the protecting canopy, whose waving blossoms were reflected on the fountain, Flodoardo was seated, and fixt his eyes on a roll of parchment.

Rosabella hesitated whether she should retire or stay. Flodoardo started from his place apparently in no less confusion than herself, and relieved her from her indecision by taking her hand with respect, and conducting her to the seat which he had just quitted.

Now then she could not possibly retire

tire immediately, unless she meant to violate every common principle of good breeding.

Her hand was still clasped in Flodoardo's—But it was so natural for him to take it, that she could not blame him for having done so.—But what was she next to do? Draw her hand away? Why should she, since he did her hand no harm by ke ping it, and the keeping it seemed to make him so happy? And how could the gentle Rosabella resolve to commit an act of such unheard of cruelty, as wilfully to deprive any one of a pleasure which made *him* so happy and which did *herself* no harm?

—" Signora," said Flodoardo, merely for the sake of saying something, " you
do

do well to enjoy the open air: the evening is beautiful."—

—" But I interrupt your studies, my Lord?" said Rosabella.

—" By no means," answered Flodoardo; and there this interesting conversation came to a full stop.—Both looked down; both examined the heaven and the earth, the trees and the flowers, in the hopes of finding some hints for renewing the conversation; but the more anxiously they sought them, the more difficult did it seem to find what they sought: and in this painful embarrassment did two whole precious minutes elapse!

—" Ah! what a beautiful flower!" suddenly

suddenly cried Rosabella, in order to break the silence, then stooped and plucked a violet with an appearance of the greatest eagerness; though, in fact, nothing at that moment could have been more a matter of indifference.

—" It is a very beautiful flower, indeed!" gravely observed Flodoardo, and was out of all patience with himself for having made so flat a speech.

—" Nothing can surpass this purple!" continued Rosabella ; " red and blue so happily blended, that no painter could produce so perfect an union !"

—" Red and blue ? the one, the symbol of happiness, the other of affection .... Ah! Rosabella, how enviable will
be

be that man's lot on whom your hand should bestow such a flower! Happiness and affection are more inseparably united than the red and blue which purple that violet!"—

—" You seem to attach a value to the flower of which it is but little deserving."—

" Might I but know on whom Rosabella will one day bestow what that flower expresses.... Yet this is a subject, which I have no right to discuss—I know not what has happened to me to-day; I make nothing but blunders and mistakes —Forgive my presumption, Lady; I will hazard such forward inquiries no more."—

He

He was silent; Rosabella was silent also. All was calm and hushed, except in the hearts of the lovers.

But though they could forbid their lips to betray their hidden affection; though Rosabella's tongue said not— " thou art he, Flodoardo, on whom this flower should be bestowed;"—though Flodoardo's words had not exprest— " Rosabella, give me that violet and that which it implies;"——Oh! their eyes were far from being silent. Those treacherous interpreters of secret feelings acknowledged more to each other than their hearts had yet acknowledged to themselves!

Flodoardo and Rosabella gazed on each other with looks which made all
speech

speech unnecessary. Sweet, tender, and enthusiastic was the smile which played round Rosabella's lips, when her eyes met those of the youth whom she had selected from the rest of mankind; and with mingled emotions of hope and fear did the youth study the *meaning* of that smile—He understood it, and his heart beat louder, and his eyes flamed brighter.

Rosabella trembled; her eyes could no longer sustain the fire of his glances, and a modest blush overspread her face and bosom.

—" Rosabella!" at length murmured Flodoardo unconsciously, and—" Flodoardo!" sighed Rosabella in the same tone.

—" Give

—" Give *me* that violet!" he exclaimed eagerly; then sank at her feet, and in a tone of the most humble supplication repeated—" Oh! give it to *me!*"

Rosabella held the flower fast.

—" Ask for it what thou wilt; if a throne can purchase it, I will pay that price, or perish!—Rosabella, give me that flower."—

She stole one look at the handsome suppliant, and dared not hazard a second.

—" My repose, my happiness, my life, nay, even my glory, all depend on the possession of that little flower! Let *that* be mine, and here I solemnly renounce all else which the world calls precious!"

The flower trembled in her snowy hand; her fingers clasped it less firmly.

—" You hear me, Rosabella? I kneel at your feet, and am I then in vain a beggar?"—

The word *beggar* recalled to her memory Camilla and her prudent counsels—" What am I doing?" she said to herself; " have I forgotten my promise .... my resolution.... Fly, Rosabella, fly, or this hour makes you faithless to yourself and duty!"—

She

She tore the flower to pieces, and threw it contemptuously on the ground.

—" I understand you, Flodoardo," said she, " and having understood you, will never suffer this subject to be renewed. Here let us part, and let me not again be offended by a similar presumption—Farewell!"—

She turned from him with disdain, and left Flodoardo rooted to his place with sorrow and astonishment.

CHAP. V.

The Assassin.

Scarcely had she reached her chamber, ere Rosabella repented her having acted so courageously. It was cruel in her, she thought, to have given him so harsh an answer! She recollected with what hopeless and melancholy looks the poor thunderstruck youth had followed her steps as she turned to leave him. She fancied that she saw him stretched despairing on the earth, his hair dishevelled,

velled, his eyes filled with tears. She heard him term her the murderess of his repose, pray for death, as his only refuge, and she saw him with every moment approach towards the attainment of his prayer, through the tears which he shed on *her* account. Already she heard those dreadful words—" Flodoardo is no more!"—Already she saw the sympathizing multitude weep round the tomb of him, whom all the virtuous loved, and whom the wicked dreaded; whom all his friends adored, and whom even his enemies admired.

—" Alas! alas!" cried she, " this was but a wretched attempt to play the heroine; already does my resolution fail me. Ah! Flodoardo, I meant not what I said! I love you, love you now, and must love you always, though Camilla may chide, and though my good uncle may hate me."—

In a few days after this interview, she understood that an extraordinary alteration had taken place in Flodoardo's manner and appearance; that he had withdrawn himself from all general society; and that when the solicitations of his intimate friends compelled him to appear in their circle, his spirits seemed evidently deprest by the weight of an unconquerable melancholy.

This intelligence was like the stroke of a poniard to the feeling heart of Rosabella. She fled for shelter to the solitude of her chamber, there indulged her feelings without restraint, and lamented, with

with showers of repentant tears, her harsh treatment of Flodoardo.

The grief which preyed in secret on her soul, soon undermined her health No one could relieve her sufferings, for no one knew the cause of her melancholy, or the origin of her illness. No wonder then that Rosabella's situation at length excited the most bitter anxiety in the bosom of her venerable uncle. No wonder, too, that Flodoardo entirely withdrew himself from a world, which was become odious to him since Rosabella was to be seen in it no longer; and that he devoted himself in solitude to the indulgence of a passion, which he had vainly endeavoured to subdue; and which, in the impetuosity of its course,

had

had already swallowed up every other wish, and every other sentiment.

But let us for a moment turn from the sick chamber of Rosabella, and visit the dwellings of the conspirators, who were now advancing with rapid strides towards the execution of their plans; and who, with every hour that past over their heads, became more numerous, more powerful, and more dangerous to Andreas and his beloved republic.

Parozzi, Memmo, Contarino, and Falieri [the chiefs of this desperate undertaking] now assembled frequently in the Cardinal Gonzaga's palace, where the different plans for altering the constitution of Venice were brought forward and discussed.

discussed. But in all these different schemes it was evident that the proposer was solely actuated by considerations of private interest—The object of one was to get free from the burthen of enormous debts; another was willing to sacrifice every thing to gratify his inordinate ambition; the cupidity of *this* man was excited by the treasures of Andreas and his friends; while *that* was actuated by resentment of some fancied offence, a resentment which could only be quenched with the offender's blood.

These execrable wretches, who aimed at nothing less than the total overthrow of Venice, or at least of her government, looked towards the completion of their extravagant hopes with the greater confidence, since a new but necessary addition to the already-existing taxes had put the Venetian populace out of humour with their rulers.

Rich enough, both in adherents and in wealth, to realize their fearful projects; rich enough in bold, shrewd, desperate men, whose minds were all adapted to the contrivance and execution of revolutionary projects; they now looked down with contempt on the good old Doge, who as yet entertained no suspicion of the object of their nocturnal meetings.

Still did they not dare to carry their projects into effect till some principal persons in the state should be prevented by *death* from throwing obstacles in their way. For the accomplishment of this
part

part of their plan they relied on the daggers of the banditti. Dreadful therefore was the sound in their ears when the bell gave the signal for execution, and they saw their best-founded hopes expire on the scaffold which supported the headless trunks of the four Bravos. But if their consternation was great at thus losing the destined instruments of their designs, how extravagant was their joy when the proud Abellino dared openly to declare to Venice, that he still inhabited the republic, and that he still wore a dagger at the disposal of Vice.

—" This desperado is the very man for us!" they exclaimed unanimously, and in rapture; and now their most ardent wish was to enroll Abellino in their service.

That

That object was soon attained—they sought the daring ruffian, and he suffered himself to be found. He visited their meetings, but in his promises and demands he was equally extravagant.

The first and most earnest wish of the whole conspiracy was the death of Conari, the procurator; a man whom the Doge valued beyond all others; a man, whose eagle-eyes made the conspirators hourly tremble for their secret, and whose services the Doge had accepted, in preference to those of the Cardinal Gonzaga.—But the sum which Abellino demanded for the murder of this one man was enormous.

—" Give me the reward which I require;" said he, " and I promise, on the

the word of a man of honour, that after this night the procurator Conari shall give you no further trouble. Exalt him to heaven, or imprison him in hell, I'll engage to find, and stab him."

What could they do? Abellino was not a man to be easily beat down in his demands. The Cardinal was impatient to attain the summit of his wishes; but his road lay straight over Conari's grave!

Abellino received the sum demanded; the next day the venerable Conari, the Doge's best and dearest friend, the pride and safeguard of the republic, was no longer numbered among the living.

—" 'Tis a terrible fellow, this Abellino!" cried the conspirators when the news

news reached them, and celebrated the Procurator's death in triumph at the Cardinal's midnight feast.

The Doge was almost distracted with terror and astonishment. He engaged to give ten thousand sequins to any one who should discover by whom Conari had been removed from the world. A proclamation to this effect was published at the corner of every street in Venice, and made known throughout the territories of the republic. A few da ysafter this proclamation had been made, a paper was discovered affixed to the principal door of the Venetian Signoria.

VENETIANS!

You would fain know the author of Conari's death: to spare you much fruitless

less trouble, I hereby acknowledge, that I, Abellino, was his assassin. Twice did I bury my dagger in his heart, and then sent his body to feed fishes. The Doge promises *ten* thousand sequins to him who shall *discover* Conari's murderer; and to him who shall be clever enough to *seize* him, Abellino hereby promises *twenty*—Adieu, Signors; I remain your faithful servant,

ABELLINO.

CHAP. VI.

The two greatest Men in Venice.

It must be superfluous to inform my readers that all Venice became furious at this new insolence. Within the memory of man had no one ever treated with such derision the celebrated Venetian police, or set the Doge's power at defiance with such proud temerity. This occurrence threw the whole city into confusion; every one was on the look out; the patroles were doubled; the
sbirri

sbirri extended their researches on all sides; yet no one could see, or hear, or discover the most distant trace of Abellino.

The priests in their sermons strove to rouze the slumbering vengeance of Heaven to crush this insolent offender. The ladies were ready to swoon at the very name of Abellino, for who could assure them that, at some unexpected moment, he might not pay *them* the same compliment which he had paid to Rosabella? As for the old women, they unanimously asserted, that Abellino had sold himself to the Prince of Darkness, by whose assistance he was enabled to sport with the patience of all pious Venetians, and deride the impotence of their just indignation. The Cardinal and his associates were

were proud of their terrible confederate, and looked forward with confidence to the triumphant issue of their undertaking. The deserted family of Conari called down curses on his murderer's head, and wished that their tears might be changed into a sea of sulphur, in whose waves they might plunge the monster Abellino: nor did Conari's relations feel more grief for his loss than the Doge and his two confidents, who swore never to rest till they had discovered the lurking-place of the ruthless assassin, and had punished his crime with tenfold vengeance.

—" Yet, after all," said Andreas one evening, as he sat alone in his private chamber, " after all, it must be confest that this Abellino is a singular man———

He

He who can do what Abellino has done, must possess both such talents and such courage as [stood he at the head of an army] would enable him to conquer half the world!—Would that I could once get a sight of him!"—

—" Look up then!" roared Abellino, and clapped the Doge on the shoulder—Andreas started from his seat. A colossal figure stood before him, wrapt in a dark mantle, above which appeared a countenance so hideous and forbidding, that the universe could not have produced its equal.

—" Who art thou?" stammered out the Doge.

—" Thou seest me, and canst doubt?

P

Well

Well then! I am *Abellino*, the good friend of your murdered Conari, and the republic's most submissive slave."—

The brave Andreas, who had never trembled in fight by land or by sea, and for whom no danger had possest terrors sufficient to shake his undaunted resolution, the brave Andreas now forgot for a few moments his usual presence of mind. Speechless did he gaze on the daring assassin, who stood before him calm and haughty, unappalled by the majesty of the greatest man in Venice.

Abellino nodded to him with an air of familiar protection, and graciously condescended to grin upon him with a kind of half-friendly smile.

—" Abellino,"

—" Abellino," said the Doge at length, endeavouring to recollect himself, " thou art a fearful.... a detestable man!"

—" Fearful?" answered the Bravo; " Dost *thou* think me so? Good! that glads me to my very heart!—Detestable? that may be so, or it may not. I confess the sign which I hang out gives no great promise of good entertainment within; but yet, Andreas, one thing is certain— You and I stand on the same line, for at this moment we are the two greatest men in Venice; *you* in your way, *I* in mine."—

The Doge could not help smiling at the Bravo's familiar tone.

—" Nay,

—" Nay, nay!" continued Abellino; " no smiles of disbelief, if you please. Allow me, though a Bravo, to compare myself to a Doge; truly I think there's no great presumption in placing myself on a level with a man, whom I hold in my power, and who therefore is in fact beneath me."—

The Doge made a movement, as would he have left him.

—" Not so fast," said Abellino laughing rudely, and he barred the Doge's passage. " Accident seldom unites in so small a space as this chamber a pair of such great men—Stay where you are, for I have not done with you yet: we must have a little conversation."—

—" Hear

—" Hear me, Abellino!" said the Doge, mustering up all the dignity which he possest; " thou hast received great talents from Nature: why dost thou employ them to so little advantage? I here promise you, on my most sacred word, pardon for the past, and protection for the future, will you but name to me the villain who bribed you to assassinate Conari, abjure your bloody trade, and accept an honest employment in the service of the republic.——If this offer is rejected, at least quit with all speed the territory of Venice, or I swear.."—

" Ho! ho!" interrupted Abellino; " *pardon* and *protection*, say you? It is long since I thought it worth my while to care for such trifles—Abellino is able to protect himself without foreign aid; and

and as to pardon, mortals cannot give absolution for sins like mine. On that day when all men must give in the list of their offences, then too will *I* give in *mine*, but till then *never*—You would know the name of him who bribed me to be Conari's murderer? Well, well; you shall know it.... but not to-day.— I must quit with all speed the Venetian territory? and wherefore? through fear of thee?—Ho! ho! through fear of Venice? Ha! Abellino fears not Venice; 'tis Venice that fears Abellino!—You would have me abjure my profession?— Well, Andreas, there is one condition which perhaps......"—

—" Name it!" cried the Doge eagerly; " will ten thousand sequins purchase

chase your departure from the republic?"—

—" I would gladly give you twice as much myself, could you recall the insult of offering Abellino so miserable a bribe! —No, Andreas, but one price can pay me: give me your niece for my bride; I love Rosabella, the daughter of Guiscard of Corfu."—

—" Monster!—what insolence.."

—" Ho! ho!—Patience, patience, good uncle that is to be! Will you accept my terms?"—

—" Name what sum can satisfy you, and it shall be yours this instant, so you will only relieve Venice from your presence,

sence. Though it should cost the republic a million, she will be a gainer, if her air is no longer poisoned by your breath."—

—" Indeed?—Why in fact a million is not so great a sum; for, look ye, Andreas, I have just sold for near *half* a million the lives of your two dear friends, Manfrone and Lomellino.—Now give me Rosabella, and I break the bargain."—

—" Miscreant! Has Heaven no lightnings......"—

—" You will not?—Mark me! In four-and-twenty hours shall Manfrone and Lomellino be food for fishes—— Abellino has said it!—Away!"

And

And with these words he drew a pistol from under his cloak, and flashed it in the Doge's face—Blinded by the powder, and confused by the unexpected explosion, Andreas started back, and sank bewildered on a neighbouring sofa—He soon recovered from his astonishment; he sprang from his seat to summon his guards, and seize Abellino——But Abellino had already disappeared.

On that same evening were Parozzi and his confederates assembled in the palace of the Cardinal Gonzaga. The table was spread with the most luxurious profusion, and they arranged over their flowing goblets plans for the republic's ruin—The Cardinal related how he had of late contrived to insinuate himself into the Doge's good graces, and had succeeded

ceeded in impressing him with an opinion that the chiefs of the confederacy were fit men to hold offices of important trust. Contarino boasted that he doubted not before long to be appointed to the vacant Procuratorship. Parozzi reckoned, for *his* share, upon Rosabella's hand, and the place either of Lomellino or Manfrone, when once those two chief obstacles to his hopes should be removed. Such was the conversation in which they were engaged, when the clock struck twelve, the doors flew wide, and Abellino stood before them!

—" Wine there!" cried he; " the work is done—Manfrone and Lomellino are at supper with the worms."—

All sprang from their seats in rapture and astonishment.

—" And I have thrown the Doge himself into such a fit of terror, that I warrant you he will not recover himself easily.—Now answer; are you content with me, you blood-hounds?"—

—" Next then for Flodoardo!" shouted Parozzi.

—" Flodoardo?" muttered Abellino between his teeth; " hum! hum!—that's not so easy.

End of Book the Second.

BOOK THE THIRD

CHAP. I.

The Lovers.

ROSABELLA, the idol of all Venice, lay on the bed of sickness; a sorrow, whose cause was carefully concealed from every one, undermined her health, and destroyed the bloom of her beauty. She loved the noble Flodoardo; and who could have known Flodoardo and *not* have loved him?—His majestic stature, his expressive countenance, his enthusiastic

astic glance, his whole being declared aloud—" Flodoardo is Nature's favourite!"—and Rosabella had been always a great admirer of Nature.

But if Rosabella was ill, Flodoardo was scarcely better. He confined himself to his own apartment; he shunned society, and frequently made long journies to different cities of the republic, in hopes of distracting his thoughts by change of place from that object, which, wherever he went, still pursued him. He had now been absent for three whole weeks. No one knew in what quarter he was wandering; and it was during this absence that the so long expected Prince of Monaldeschi arrived at Venice, to claim Rosabella as his bride.

His

His appearance, to which a month before Andreas looked forward with such pleasing expectation, now afforded but little satisfaction to the Doge. Rosabella was too ill to receive her suitor's visits, and he did not allow her much time to recover her health; for six days after his arrival at Venice, the Prince was found murdered in a retired part of one of the public gardens. His sword lay by him, unsheathed and bloody; his tablets were gone, but one leaf had been torn from them and fastened on his breast—It was examined, and found to contain the following lines apparently written in blood:

—" Let no one pretend to Rosabella's hand who is not prepared to share the fate

fate of Monaldeschi!——The Bravo
" ABELLINO."

—" Oh! where shall I now fly for comfort! for protection!" exclaimed the Doge in despair when this dreadful news was announced—" Why, why is Flodoardo absent?"—

Anxiously did he now desire the youth's return, to support him under the weight of these heavy misfortunes; nor was it long before that desire was gratified—Flodoardo returned.

—" Welcome, noble youth!" said the Doge, when he saw the Florentine enter his apartment; " you must not in future deprive me of your presence for so long. I am now a poor, forsaken old man

man—You have heard that Lomellino .... that Manfrone...."—

—" I know all!" answered Flodoardo with a melancholy air.

—" Satan has burst his chains, and now inhabits Venice under the name of Abellino, robbing me of all that my soul holds precious. Flodoardo, for heaven's love be cautious; often, during your absence, have I trembled lest the miscreant's dagger should have deprived me too of *you*. I have much to say to you, my young friend, but I must defer it till the evening; a foreigner of consequence has appointed this hour for an audience, and I must hasten to receive him—But in the evening...."

He

He was interrupted by the appearance of Rosabella, who, with tottering steps and pale cheeks, advanced slowly into the apartment. She saw Flodoardo, and a faint blush overspread her countenance. Flodoardo rose from his seat, and welcomed her with an air of distant respect.

—" Do not go yet," said the Doge; " perhaps in half an hour I may be at liberty—In the mean while I leave you to entertain my poor Rosabella : she has been very ill during your absence, and I am still uneasy about her health. She kept her bed till yesterday, and truly I think she has still left it too soon."—

The venerable Doge quitted the apartment, and the lovers once more found
themselves

themselves alone. Rosabella drew near the window; Flodoardo at length ventured to approach it also.

—" Signora," said he, " are you still angry with me ?"—

—" I am not angry with you," stammered out Rosabella, and blushed as she recollected the garden-scene.

—" And you have quite forgiven my transgression ?"—

—" Your transgression ?" repeated Rosabella with a faint smile; " yes; if it *was* a transgression, I have *quite* forgiven it. Dying people ought to pardon those who have trespassed against them, in order that they, in their turn, may be pardoned

pardoned their trespasses against Heaven—and *I* am dying; I feel it!"

—" Signora!"—

—" Nay, 'tis past a doubt—It's true I have quitted my sick bed since yesterday; but I know well that I am soon to return to it, never to leave it more.—And therefore.... therefore I now ask your pardon, Signor, for the vexation which I was obliged to cause to you the last time we met."—

Flodoardo replied not.

—" Will you not forgive me?—You must be very difficult to appease...... very revengeful!"—

Flodoardo fixed his eyes on her countenance with a melancholy smile—Rosabella extended her hand towards him—

—" Will you refuse my offered hand? Shall all be forgotten?"—

—" Forgotten, Lady? Never! never!—Every word and look of yours is stamped on my memory, never to be effaced. I cannot forget a transaction in which *you* bore a part; I cannot forget the scene that past between us, every circumstance is too precious and sacred. —As to *pardon*"....—He took her extended hand, and prest it respectfully to his lips—" I would to Heaven, dear Lady, that you had in truth injured me much, that I might have much to forgive

give you—Alas! I have at present nothing to pardon."—

Both were now silent; at length Rosabella resumed the conversation by saying—" You have made a long absence from Venice: did you travel far?"

—" I did."—

—" And received much pleasure from your journey?"—

—" Much; for every where I heard the praises of Rosabella."—

—" Count Flodoardo!"—she interrupted him with a look of reprehension, but in a gentle voice, " would you again offend me?"—

—" That

—" That will soon be out of my power—Perhaps you can guess what are my present intentions."—

—" To resume your travels soon?"—

—" Exactly so; and the next time that I quit Venice, to return to it no more."—

—" No more?" she repeated eagerly; " Oh! not so, Flodoardo! Ah! can you leave me?"—She stopped, ashamed of her imprudence—" Can you leave my uncle, I meant to say? You do but jest, I doubt not."—

—" By my honour, Lady, I never was more in *earnest*."—

—" And

—" And whither then do you mean to go?"—

—" To Malta, and assist the knights in their attacks upon the Corsairs of Barbary. Providence perhaps may enable me to obtain the command of a galley; then will I call my vessel ' Rosabella;'—then shall the war-cry be still ' Rosabella;' that name will render me invincible!"

—" Oh! this is mockery, Count; I have not deserved that you should sport with my feelings so cruelly."—

—" It is to *spare* your feelings, Signora, that I am now resolved to fly from Venice; my presence might cause you some uneasy moments. I am not the

happy

happy man whose sight is destined to give you pleasure; I will at least avoid giving you pain."—

—" And you really can resolve to abandon the Doge, whose esteem for you is so sincere, whose friendship has always been so warm?"—

—" I value his friendship highly; but it is not sufficient to make me happy—and could he lay kingdoms at my feet, still would his friendship be insufficient to make me happy."—

—" Does then your happiness require so much?"—

—" It does; much more than I have mentioned, infinitely more!—But one boon

boon can make me happy—I have begged for it on my knees."—He caught her hand, and prest it eagerly to his lips—" I have begged for it, Rosabella, ... and my suit has been rejected!"—

—" You are a strange enthusiast!" she said with difficulty, and scarcely knew what she said; while Flodoardo drew her gently nearer to him, and murmured in a supplicating voice—" Rosabella!"—

—" What would you of me?"—

—" My happiness!"—

She gazed upon him for a moment undecided, then hastily drew away her hand, and exclaimed—" Leave me this moment,

moment, I command you! Leave me, for Heaven's sake!"—

Flodoardo clasped his hands together in despair and anguish—he bowed his head in token of obedience; he left her with slow steps and a melancholy air, and as he past the threshold, turned to bid her farewell for ever. Suddenly she rushed towards him, caught his hand, and prest it to her heart.

—" Flodoardo!" she cried, " I am thine!" and sank motionless at his feet.

CHAP. II.

A dangerous promise.

And now who was so blest as the fortunate Flodoardo? The victory was his own; he had heard the wished-for sentence pronounced by the lips of Rosabella—He raised her from the ground, and placed her on a sopha—Her blue eyes soon unclosed themselves once more, and the first object which they beheld was Flodoardo kneeling at her feet, while with one arm he encircled
her

her waist. Her head sank upon the shoulder of the man for whom she had wept so many tears, for whom she had breathed so many sighs, who had occupied so many of her thoughts by day, who had been present in so many of her dreams by night.

As they gazed in silent rapture on each other, they forgot that they were mortals : they seemed to be transported to an happier, better world. Rosabella thought that the chamber in which she sat was transformed into an earthly Paradise ; invisible seraphs seemed to hallow by their protecting presence the indulgence of her innocent affection ; and she poured forth her secret thanks to Him who had given her an heart susceptible of love.

Through

Through the whole course of man's existence such a moment as this occurs but once. Happy is he who sighs for its arrival; happy is he who when it arrives has a soul worthy of its enjoyment; happy is even he for whom that moment has long been past, so it past not unenjoyed, for the recollection of it still is precious. Sage philosophers, in vain do you assure us that the raptures of a moment like this are mere illusions of an heated imagination, scarcely more solid than an enchanting dream, which fades before the sunbeams of truth and reason. Alas! does there exist an happiness under the moon which owes not its charms in some degree to the magic of imagination?

—" You are dear to me, Flodoardo!"
murmured

murmured Rosabella, for Camilla and her counsels were quite forgotten; " oh! you are very, very dear!"—

The youth only thanked her by clasping her still closer to his bosom, while, for the first time, he sealed her coral lips with his own.

At that moment the door was suddenly thrown open; the Doge Andreas re-entered the apartment; the expected stranger had been suddenly taken ill, and Andreas was no sooner at liberty than he hastened to rejoin his favourite. The rustling of his garments rouzed the lovers from their dream of bliss. Rosabella started from Flodoardo's embrace with a cry of terror; Flodoardo quitted his

his kneeling posture, yet seemed by no means disconcerted at the discovery.

Andreas gazed upon them for some minutes, with a look which exprest at once anger, melancholy, and the most heart-felt disappointment. He sighed deeply, cast his eyes towards heaven, and in silence turned to leave the apartment.

—" Stay yet one moment, noble Andreas!" cried the Florentine.

The Doge turned, and Flodoardo threw himself at his feet. Andreas looked down with calm and serious dignity on the kneeling offender, by whom his friendship had been unworthily rewarded,

warded, and by whom his confidence had been so cruelly betrayed.

—" Young man," said he in a stern voice, " the attempt to excuse yourself must be fruitless."—

—" Excuse myself?" interrupted Flodoardo boldly; " no, my Lord, I need no excuses for loving Rosabella; 'twere for him to excuse himself who had seen Rosabella and *not* loved her— yet if it is indeed a crime in me that I adore Rosabella. . . . 'tis a crime of which Heaven itself will absolve me, since it formed Rosabella so worthy to be adored!"—

—" You seem to lay too much stress on

on this fantastic apology," answered the Doge contemptuously; " at least, you cannot expect that it should have much weight with me."—

—" I say it once more, my Lord," resumed Flodoardo, while he rose from the ground, " that I intend to make *no* apology. I mean not to excuse my love for Rosabella, but to request your approbation of that love—Andreas, I adore your niece; I demand her for my bride."—

The Doge started in astonishment at this bold and unexpected request.

—" It is true," continued the Florentine, " I am no more than a needy, unknown youth, and it seems a piece of strange

strange temerity when such a man proposes himself to espouse the heiress of the Venetian Doge. But, by heaven, I am confident that the great Andreas means not to bestow his Rosabella on one of those whose claims to favour are overflowing coffers, extensive territories, and sounding titles, or who vainly decorate their insignificance with the glory obtained by their ancestors; glory of which they are themselves incapable of acquiring a single ray. I acknowledge freely that I have as yet performed no actions which make me deserving such a reward as Rosabella; but it shall not be long ere I *will* perform such actions, or perish in the attempt."—

The Doge turned from him with a look of displeasure.

—" Oh!

—" Oh! be not incensed with him, dear uncle!" said Rosabella: she hastened to detain the Doge, threw her white arms round his neck fondly, and concealed in his bosom the tears with which her countenance was bedewed.

—" Make your demands!" continued Flodoardo, still addressing himself to the Doge; " say what you wish me to do, and what you would have me become, in order to obtain from you the hand of Rosabella. Ask what you will, I will look on the task, however difficult, as nothing more than sport and pastime. By heaven, I would that Venice were at this moment exposed to the most imminent danger, and that ten thousand daggers were unsheathed against your life;

life; Rosabella my reward, how certain should I be to rescue Venice, and strike the ten thousand daggers down."—

—" I have served the republic faithfully and fervently for many a long year," answered Andreas with a bitter smile; " I have risqued my life without hesitation; I have shed my blood with profusion; I asked nothing for my reward but to pass my old age in soft tranquillity, and of this reward have I been cheated. My bosom-friends, the companions of my youth, the confidents of my age, have been torn from me by the daggers of banditti—and you, Flodoardo, you on whom I heaped all favours, have now deprived me of this, my only last remaining comfort.—Answer me, Rosabella;

bella; hast thou in truth bestowed thy heart on Flodoardo *irrevocably?*"—

One hand of Rosabella's still rested on her uncle's shoulder; with the other she clasped Flodoardo's, and prest it fondly against her heart—Yet Flodoardo seemed still unsatisfied. No sooner had the Doge's question struck his ear, than his countenance became dejected; and though his hand returned the pressure of Rosabella's, he shook his head mournfully, with an air of doubt, and cast on her a penetrating look, as would he have read the secrets of her inmost soul.

Andreas withdrew himself gently from Rosabella's arm, and for some time paced the apartment slowly, with a countenance sad and earnest. Rosabella sank upon a sopha which stood near her, and wept. Flodoardo eyed the Doge, and waited for his decision with impatience.

Thus past some minutes. An awful silence reigned through the chamber: Andreas seemed to be labouring with some resolution of dreadful importance. The lovers wished, yet dreaded, the conclusion of the scene, and with every moment their anxiety became more painful.

—" Flodoardo!" at length said the Doge, and suddenly stood still in the middle of the chamber. Flodoardo advanced with a respectful air—" Young man," he continued, " I am at length resolved; Rosabella loves you, nor will I oppose the decision of her heart: but
Rosabella

Rosabella is much too precious to admit of my bestowing her on the first who thinks fit to demand her—the man to whom I give her, must be worthy such a gift: she must be the reward of his services, nor can he do services so great that such a reward will not overpay them.—Your claims on the republic's gratitude are as yet but trifling; an opportunity now offers of rendering us an essential service—The murderer of Conari, Manfrone, and Lomellino. . . . Go, bring him hither!—Alive or dead, thou must bring to this palace the terrible banditti-king, *Abellino!*" —

At this unexpected conclusion of a speech, on which his happiness or despair depended, Flodoardo started back; the colour fled from his cheeks.

—" My noble Lord!" he said at length hesitating; " you know well that...."—

—" I know well," interrupted Andreas, " how difficult a task I enjoin, when I require the delivery of Abellino. For myself I swear, that I had rather a thousand times force my passage with a single vessel through the whole Turkish fleet, and carry off the admiral's ship from the midst of them, than attempt to seize this Abellino, who seems to have entered into a compact with Lucifer himself; who is to be found every where and no where; whom so many have seen, but whom no one knows; whose cautious subtilety has brought to shame the vigilance of our State-inquisitors, of the College of Ten, and of all their legions

gions of spies and sbirri; whose very name strikes terror into the hearts of the bravest Venetians, and from whose dagger I myself am not safe upon my throne!—I know well, Flodoardo, how much I ask; but I know also how much I proffer.—You seem irresolute?—You are silent?—Flodoardo, I have long watched you with attention; I have discovered in you marks of a superior genius, and therefore am I induced to make such a demand. If any one is able to cope with Abellino, thou art the man——I wait your answer."—

Flodoardo paced the chamber in silence. Dreadful was the enterprize proposed: woe to him should Abellino discover his purpose!—But Rosabella was the reward! He cast a look on the
beloved-

beloved-one, and resolved to risque every thing.

He advanced towards the Doge.

Andreas—Now then, Flodoardo? Your resolution?

Flodoardo—Should I deliver Abellino into your power, do you solemnly swear that Rosabella shall be my bride?

Andreas—She shall; and *not till then*.

Rosabella—Ah! Flodoardo, I fear this undertaking will end fatally. Abellino is so crafty.... so dreadful...... Oh! look well to yourself, for should you meet

meet with this detested monster, whose dagger. . . .

Flodoardo—[interrupting her hastily] —Oh! silence, Rosabella!—at least allow me to hope!—Noble Andreas, give me your hand, and pledge your princely word that Abellino once in your power, nothing shall prevent me from being Rosabella's husband.

Andreas—I swear it; deliver into my power, either alive or dead, this most dangerous foe of Venice, and nothing shall prevent Rosabella from being your wife. In pledge of which I here give you my princely hand.

Flodoardo grasped the Doge's hand in silence, and shook it thrice. He turned

turned to Rosabella, and seemed on the point of addressing her, when he suddenly turned away, struck his forehead, and measured the apartment with disordered and unsteady steps. The clock in the tower of St. Mark's church struck *five.*

—" Time flies!" cried Flodoardo; " no more delay then. In four-and-twenty hours will I produce in this very palace this dreaded bravo, Abellino."—

Andreas shook his head—" Young man," said he, " be less confident in your promises; I shall have more faith in your performance."

Flodoardo—[serious and firm]—Let things terminate as they may, either I will

will keep my word, or never again will cross the threshold of your palace—I have discovered some traces of the miscreant, and I trust that I shall amuse you to-morrow, at this time and in this place, with the representation of a comedy; but should it prove a tragedy instead, God's will be done.

Andreas—Remember, that too much haste is dangerous: rashness will destroy even the frail hopes of success, which you may reasonably indulge at present.

Flodoardo—Rashness, my Lord? He who has lived as *I* have lived, and suffered what *I* have suffered, must have been long since cured of rashness.

Rosabella—[taking his hand]—Yet
be

be not too confident of your own strength, I beseech you! Dear Flodoardo, my uncle loves you, and his advice is wise! Beware of Abellino's dagger!

Flodoardo—The best way to escape his dagger is not to allow him time to use it: within four-and-twenty hours must the deed be done, or never.—Now then, illustrious Prince, I take my leave of you; to-morrow I doubt not to convince you that nothing is too much for love to venture.

Andreas—Right; to *venture* ;—but to *achieve?*

Flodoardo—Ah! that must depend ......—He paused suddenly; again his eyes were fastened eagerly on those of Rosabella;

Rosabella; and it was evident that with every moment his uneasiness acquired fresh strength—He resumed his discourse to Andreas, with a movement of impatience.

—" Noble Andreas," said he, " do not make me dispirited;—rather let me try whether I cannot inspire you with more confidence of my success. I must first request you to order a splendid entertainment to be prepared. At this hour in the afternoon of to-morrow let me find all the principal persons in Venice, both men and women, assembled in this chamber; for, should my hopes be realized, I would willingly have spectators of my triumph. Particularly, let the venerable members of the College of Ten be invited, in order that they may
at

at last be brought face to face with this terrible Abellino, against whom they have so long been engaged in fruitless warfare.

Andreas—[after eyeing him some time with a look of mingled surprize and uncertainty]—They shall be present.

Flodoardo—I understand also, that since Conari's death you have been reconciled to the Cardinal Gonzaga; and that he has convinced you how unjust were the prejudices with which Conari had inspired you against the nobili Parozzi, Contarino, and the rest of that society—During my late excursions I have heard much in praise of these young men, which makes me wish to show

show myself to them in a favourable light—If you have no objection, let me beg you to invite them also.

Andreas—You shall be gratified.

Flodoardo—One thing more, which had nearly escaped my memory.—Let no one know the motive of this entertainment, till the whole company is assembled. Then let guards be placed around the palace, and indeed it may be as well to place them even before the doors of this saloon; for in truth this Abellino is such a desperate villain, that too many precautions cannot be taken against him. The centinels must have their pieces loaded; and, above all things, they must be strictly charged, on pain of death.

death, to let every one *enter*, but no one *quit* the chamber.

Andreas—All this shall be done punctually.

Flodoardo—I have nothing more to say—Noble Andreas, farewell.—Rosabella.... To-morrow, when the clock strikes *five*, we shall meet again, or *never!*"—

He said, and rushed out of the apartment—Andreas shook his head; while Rosabella sank upon her uncle's bosom, and wept bitterly.

CHAP. III.

The midnight meeting.

—" Victory!" shouted Parozzi as he rushed into the Cardinal Gonzaga's chamber, where the chief conspirators were all assembled; " our work goes on bravely ! Flodoardo returned this morning to Venice, and Abellino has already received the required sum."

Gonzaga—Flodoardo does not want talents ; I had rather he should live and
join

join our party. He is seldom off his guard....

Parozzi—Such vagabonds may well be cautious ; *they* must not forget themselves who have so much to conceal from others.

Falieri—Rosabella, as I understand, by no means sees this Florentine with unfavourable eyes.

Parozzi—Oh! wait till to-morrow, and then he may make love to the devil and his grandmother, if he likes it—Abellino by that time will have wrung his neck round, I warrant you!

Contarino—It is strange, that in spite of all enquiries I can learn but little at Florence

Florence respecting this Flodoardo. My letters inform me that some time ago there *did* exist a family of that name; but it has been long extinct, or if any of its descendants are still in being, at Florence their existence is quite a secret.

Gonzaga—Are you *all* invited to the Doge's to-morrow?

Contarino—All of us without exception.

Gonzaga—That is well; it seems that my recommendations have obtained some weight with him, since his triumvirate has been removed—And in the evening a masked ball is to be given; did not the Doge's Chamberlain say so?

Falieri—He did.

Memmo—I only hope there is no trick in all this—If he should have been given an hint of our conspiracy......
Mercy on us, my teeth chatter at the thought.

Gonzaga—Absurd! By what means should our designs have been made known to him? The thing is impossible!

Memmo—Impossible? What! when there's scarce a cut-purse, house-breaker, or vagabond in Venice who has not been enlisted in our service, would it be so strange if the Doge discovered a little of the business? A secret which is known to so many, how should it escape his penetration?

Contarino

Contarino — Simpleton! the same thing happens to *him*, which happens to betrayed husbands : every one can see the horns except the man who carries them. And yet I confess it is full time that we should realize our projects, and prevent the possibility of our being betrayed.

Falieri—You are right, friend; every thing is ready, and now the sooner that the blow is struck the better.

Parozzi—Nay, the discontented populace, which at present sides with us, would be perfectly well-pleased if the sport began this very night; delay the business longer, and their anger against Andreas will cool, and render them unfit for our purposes.

Contarino—Then let us decide the game at once; be to-morrow the important day! Leave the Doge to *my* disposal; I'll at least engage to bury my poniard in his heart, and then let the business end as it may, one of two things must happen; either we shall rescue ourselves from all trouble and vexation, by throwing every thing into uproar and confusion, or else we shall sail with a full wind from this cursed world to another.

Parozzi—Mark me, friends; we must go armed to the Doge's entertainment.

Gonzaga—All the members of the College of Ten have been particularly invited....

Falieri

Falieri—Down with every man of them!

Memmo—Aye, aye! Fine talking! but suppose it should turn out to be " down with *ourselves?*"—

Falieri—Thou white-livered wretch! Stay at home then, and take care of your worthless existence—But if our attempt succeeds, come not to us to re-imburse you for the sums which you have already advanced. Not a sequin shall be paid you back, depend on't!

Memmo—You wrong me, Falieri; if you wish to prove my courage, draw your sword, and measure it against mine! I am as *brave* as yourself; but, thank heaven, I am not quite so hot-headed.
Gonzaga

Gonzaga—Nay, even suppose that the event should not answer our expectations; Andreas once dead, let the populace storm if it pleases; the protection of his Holiness will sanction our proceedings.

Memmo—The Pope? May we count on his protection?

Gonzaga—[throwing him a letter]—Read there, unbeliever!—The Pope, I tell you, *must* protect us, since one of our objects is profest to be the assertion of the rights of St. Peter's Chair in Venice. Pry'thee, Memmo, teaze us no more with such doubts, but let Contarino's proposal be adopted at once. Our confederates must be summoned to Parozzi's palace with all diligence, and
there

there furnished with such weapons as are necessary. Let the stroke of midnight be the signal for Contarino's quitting the ball-room, and hastening to seize the arsenal: Salviati, who commands there, is in our interests, and will throw open the gates at the first summons.

Falieri—The Admiral Adorno, as soon as he hears the alarm-bell, will immediately lead his people to our assistance.

Parozzi—Oh! our success is certain!

Contarino—Only let us take care to make the confusion as general as possible; our adversaries must be kept in the dark who are their friends and who their foes; and all but our own party must be left

left ignorant as to the authors, the origin, and the object of the uproar.

Parozzi—By heaven, I am delighted at finding the business at length so near the moment of execution!

Falieri—Parozzi, have you distributed the white ribands, by which we are to recognize our partizans?

Parozzi—That was done some days ago.

Contarino—Then there is no more necessary to be said on the subject. Comrades, fill your goblets! We will not meet again together till our work has been compleated.

Memmo

Memmo—And yet methinks it would not be unwise to consider the matter over again coolly.

Contarino—Psha! consideration and prudence have nothing to do with a rebellion: despair and rashness in this case are better counsellors. The work once begun, the constitution of Venice once boldly overturned, so that no one can tell who is master and who is subject, *then* consideration will be of service in instructing us how far it may be necessary for our interests to push the confusion.—Come, friends! fill, fill, I say!—I cannot help laughing when I reflect that, by giving this entertainment to-morrow, the Doge himself kindly affords us an opportunity of executing our plans!

Parozzi

Parozzi—As to Flodoardo, I look upon him as already in his grave; yet before we go to-morrow to the Doge's, it will be as well to have a conference with Abellino.

Contarino—That care we will leave to you, Parozzi, and in the mean while here's the health of Abellino!

All—Abellino!

Gonzaga—And success to our enterprize to-morrow.

Memmo—I'll drink *that* toast with all my heart.

All—Success to to-morrow's enterprize!
Parozzi

Parozzi—The wine tastes well, and every face looks gay—Pass eight-and-forty hours......and shall we look as gaily?—We separate smiling; shall we smile when two nights hence we meet again?—No matter!

CHAP. IV.

The decisive day.

The next morning every thing in Venice seemed as tranquil as if nothing more than ordinary was on the point of taking place; and yet since her first foundation, never had a more important day rose on the republic.

The inhabitants of the ducal palace were in motion early. The impatient Andreas forsook the couch on which he had

had past a sleepless and anxious night, as soon as the first sunbeams penetrated through the lattice of his chamber. Rosabella had past the hours of rest in dreams of Flodoardo, and she still seemed to be dreaming of him, even after sleep was fled. Camilla's love for her fair pupil had broken her repose; she loved Rosabella as had she been her daughter, and was aware that on this interesting day depended the love-sick girl's whole future happiness. For some time Rosabella was unusually gay; she sang to her harp the most lively airs, and jested with Camilla for looking so serious and so uneasy: but when midday approached, her spirits began to forsake her. She quitted her instrument, and paced the chamber with unsteady steps. With every succeeding hour her heart palpitated with greater pain and violence, and she trembled in expectation of the scene which was soon to take place.

The most illustrious persons in Venice already filled her uncle's palace; the afternoon so much dreaded, and yet so much desired, was come; and the Doge now desired Camilla to conduct his niece to the great saloon, where she was expected with impatience by all those who were of most consequence in the republic.

Rosabella sank on her knees before a statue of the Virgin.—" Blessed Lady!" she exclaimed with lifted hands, " have mercy on me! Let all to-day end well!"—

Pale

Pale as death did she enter the chamber, in which, on the day before, she had acknowledged her love for Flodoardo, and Flodoardo had sworn to risque his life to obtain her.—Flodoardo was not yet arrived.

The assembly was brilliant, the conversation was gay. They talked over the politics of the day, and discussed the various occurrences of Europe. The Cardinal and Contarino were engaged in a conference with the Doge, while Memmo, Parozzi, and Falieri stood silent together, and revolved the project whose execution was to take place at midnight.

The weather was dark and tempestuous. The wind roared among the waters of the canal, and the vanes of the palace-towers creaked shrilly and discordantly. One storm of rain followed hard upon another.

The clock struck four. The cheeks of Rosabella, if possible, became paler than before. Andreas whispered somewhat to his chamberlain. In a few minutes the tread of armed men seemed approaching the doors of the saloon, and soon after the clattering of weapons was heard.

Instantly a sudden silence reigned through the whole assembly. The young courtiers broke off their love-speeches abruptly, and the ladies stopped in their criticisms upon the last new fashions. The statesmen dropped their political

political discussions, and gazed on each other in silence and anxiety.

The Doge advanced slowly into the midst of the assembly. Every eye was fixed upon him. The hearts of the conspirators beat painfully.

—" Be not surprised, my friends," said Andreas, " at these unusual precautions; they relate to nothing which need interfere with the pleasures of this society. You have all heard but too much of the bravo Abellino, the murderer of the procurator Conari, and of my faithful counsellers Manfrone and Lomellino, and to whose dagger my illustrious guest the Prince of Monaldeschi has but lately fallen a victim. This miscreant, the object of aversion to

every

every honest man in Venice, to whom nothing is sacred or venerable, and who has hitherto set at defiance the whole vengeance of the republic.... Before another hour expires, perhaps this outcast of hell may stand before you in this very saloon.

All — [astonished] — Abellino?—— What? the bravo Abellino?

Gonzaga—Of his own accord?

Andreas—No; not of his own accord, in truth; but Flodoardo of Florence has undertaken to render this important service to the republic, to seize Abellino cost what it may, and conduct him hither at the risque of his life.

A Senator

A Senator—The engagement will be difficult to fulfill! I doubt much Flodoardo's keeping his promise.

Another—But if he *should* perform it, the obligation which Flodoardo will lay upon the republic will not be trifling.

A third—Nay, we shall be all his debtors, nor do I know how we can reward Flodoardo for so important a service.

Andreas—Be that my task. Flodoardo has demanded my niece in marriage; if he performs his promise, Rosabella shall be his reward.

All gazed on each other in silence,

some with looks expressing the most heart-felt satisfaction, and others with glances of envy and surprize.

Falieri—[in a low voice]—Parozzi, how will this end?

Memmo—As I live, the very idea makes me shake as if I had a fever!

Parozzi—[smiling contemptuously]—It's very likely that Abellino should suffer himself to be caught!

Contarino—Pray inform me, Signors, have any of you ever met this Abellino face to face?

Several Noblemen at once—Not I! never!

A Senator

A Senator—He is a kind of spectre, who only appears now and then, when he is least expected and desired.

Rosabella—I saw him once!—Never again shall I forget the monster!

Andreas—And my interview with him is too well known to make it needful for me to relate it.

Memmo—I have heard a thousand stories about this miscreant, the one more wonderful than the other; and for my own part, I verily believe that he is Satan himself in a human form. I must say, that I think it would be wiser not to let him be brought in among us, for he is capable of strangling us all as we stand here, one after another, without mercy!

—" Gracious

—" Gracious heaven!" screamed several of the ladies; " you don't say so? What! strangle us in this very *chamber?*"

Contarino—The principal point is, whether Flodoardo will get the better of *him*, or *he* of Flodoardo: now I would lay a heavy wager, that the Florentine will return without having finished the business.

A Senator—And *I* would engage, on the contrary, that there is but one man in Venice who is capable of seizing Abellino, and that *that* man is Flodoardo of Florence. The moment that I became acquainted with him, I prophecied that one day or other he would play a brilliant part in the annals of history.

Another

Another Senator—I think with you, Signor; never was I so much struck with a man at first sight as I was with Flodoardo.

Contarino—A thousand sequins on Abellino's not being taken.... unless death should have taken him first.

The First Senator—A thousand sequins on Flodoardo seizing him....

Andreas—And delivering him up to me, either alive or dead.

Contarino—Illustrious Signors, you are witnesses of the wager—My Lord Vitalba, there is my hand on it—A thousand sequins!

The

The Senator—Done!

Contarino—[smiling]—Many thanks for your gold, Signor: I look on it as already in my purse. Flodoardo is a clever gentleman, no doubt; yet I would advise him to take good care of himself, for he will find that Abellino knows a trick or two, or I am much mistaken.

Gonzaga—May I request your Highness to inform me, whether Flodoardo is attended by the sbirri?

Andreas—No, he is alone; near four-and-twenty hours have elapsed since he set out in pursuit of the banditti.

Gonzaga—[to Contarino, with a smile of

of triumph]—I wish you joy of your thousand sequins, Signor.

Contarino—[bowing respectfully]—Since your Excellency prophecies it, I can no longer doubt my success.

Memmo—I begin to recover myself! Well! well! Let us see the end.

Three-and-twenty hours had elapsed since Flodoardo had entered into his rash engagement; the four-and-twentieth now hastened to its completion; and yet Flodoardo came not!

CHAP. V.

The clock strikes FIVE!

The Doge became uneasy. The senator Vitalba began to tremble for his thousand sequins, and the conspirators could not restrain their spiteful laughter when Contarino gravely declared that he would gladly lose not *one* thousand sequins, but twenty, if the loss of his wager through Abellino's being captured might but secure the general safety of the republic.

—" Hark!"

—" Hark!" cried Rosabella, " the clock strikes five!"—

All listened to the chimes in the tower of St. Mark's church, and trembled as they counted the strokes. Had not Camilla supported her, Rosabella would have sank upon the ground. The destined hour was past, and still Flodoardo came not!

The venerable Andreas felt a sincere affection for the Florentine: he shuddered as he dwelt upon the probability that Abellino's dagger had prevailed.

Rosabella advanced towards her uncle as would she have spoken to him; but anxiety fettered her tongue, and tears forced themselves into her eyes. She
struggled

struggled for a while to conceal her emotions, but the effort was too much for her. She threw herself on a sopha, wrang her hands, and prayed to the God of Mercy for help and comfort.

The rest of the company either formed groupes of whisperers, or strolled up and down the apartment in evident uneasiness. They would willingly have appeared gay and unconcerned, but they found it impossible to assume even an affectation of gaiety—And thus elapsed another hour, and still Flodoardo came not.

At that moment the evening sun broke through the clouds, and a ray of its setting glory was thrown full upon the countenance of Rosabella—She started

started from the sopha, extended her arms towards the radiant orb, and exclaimed, while a smile of hope played round her lips—" God is merciful! God will have mercy too on *me!*"—

Contarino—Was it at five o'clock that Flodoardo engaged to produce Abellino? It is now a full hour beyond his time.

The senator Vitalba—Let him only produce him at last, and he may be a month beyond his time if he chuses.

Andreas—Hark!—No!—Silence! silence! Surely I hear footsteps approaching the saloon!

The words were scarcely spoken when the folding doors were thrown open, and Flodoardo

Flodoardo rushed into the room, enveloped in his mantle. His hair streamed on the air in wild disorder; a deep shade was thrown over his face by the drooping plumes of his *barrette,* from which the rain was flowing; extreme melancholy was imprest on all his features; and he threw gloomy looks around him, as he bowed his head in salutation of the assembly.

Every one crouded round him; every mouth was unclosed to question him; every eye was fixed on his face, as if eager to anticipate his answers.

—" Holy Virgin!" exclaimed Memmo, " I am afraid that...."—

—" Be silent, Signor!" interrupted Contarino

Contarino sternly; " there is nothing to be afraid of."—

—" Illustrious Venetians!" it was thus that Flodoardo at length broke silence, and he spoke with the commanding tone of a hero; " I conclude that his Highness has already made known to you the object of your being thus assembled. I come to put an end to your anxiety; but first, noble Andreas, I must once more receive the assurance that Rosabella of Corfu shall become my bride, provided I deliver into your power the bravo Abellino.

Andreas—[examining his countenance with extreme anxiety]—Flodoardo.... have you succeeded? Is Abellino your prisoner?

Flodoardo—If Abellino *is* my prisoner, shall Rosabella be my bride?

Andreas—Bring me Abellino, alive or dead, and she is yours—I swear it beyond the power of retracting, and swear also that her dowry shall be royal!

Flodoardo—Illustrious Venetians, ye have heard the Doge's oath?

All—We are your witnesses.

Flodoardo—[advancing a few paces with a bold air, and speaking in a firm voice]—Well then! Abellino *is* in my power.... is in *yours!*

All—[in confusion, and a kind of uproar]

roar]—In ours?—Merciful heaven!—Where is he?—Abellino?

Andreas—Is he dead or living?

Flodoardo—He still lives.

Gonzaga—[hastily]—He lives?

Flodoardo—[bowing to the Cardinal respectfully]—He still lives, Signor!

Rosabella—[pressing Camilla to her bosom]—Didst thou hear that, Camilla? Didst thou hear it?—The villain still lives! Not one drop of blood has stained the innocent hand of Flodoardo.

The senator Vitalba—Signor Conta-rino,

rino, I have won a thousand sequins of you.

Contarino—So it should seem, Signor!

Andreas—My son, you have bound the republic to you for ever, and I rejoice that it is to Flodoardo that she is indebted for a service so essential.

Vitalba—And permit me, noble Florentine, to thank you for this heroic act in the name of the senate of Venice —Our first care shall be to seek out a reward proportioned to your merits.

Flodoardo—[extending his arm towards Rosabella with a melancholy air]
—*There*

—*There* stands the only reward for which I wish.

Andreas—[joyfully]—And that reward is your own—But where have you left the blood-hound? Conduct him hither, my son, and let me look on him once more—When last I saw him, he had the insolence to tell me—" Doge, I am your equal; this narrow chamber now holds the two greatest men in Venice."—Now then let me see how this other great man looks in captivity.

Two or three Senators—Where is he? —Bring him hither!

Several of the ladies screamed at hearing this proposal—" For heaven's sake!" cried they, " keep the monster away from us! I shall be frightened out of my senses if he comes here!"—

—" Noble Ladies!" said Flodoardo with a smile expressing rather sorrow than joy, " you have nothing to apprehend. Abellino shall do you no harm; but he needs *must* come hither, to claim " *the Bravo's Bride.*"—And he pointed to Rosabella.

—" Oh! my best friend!" she answered, " how shall I express my thanks to you for having thus put an end to my terrors! I shall now tremble no more at hearing Abellino named; Rosabella shall now be called ' the Bravo's Bride' no longer!"—

Falieri—Is Abellino already in this palace?

Flodoardo—He is.

Vitalba—Then why do you not produce him?—Why do you trifle so long with our impatience?

Flodoardo—Be patient! It's now time that the play should begin.—Be seated, noble Andreas! Let all the rest arrange themselves behind the Doge!—*Abellino's coming!*"—

At that word both old and young, both male and female, with the rapidity of lightning flew to take shelter behind Andreas. Every heart beat anxiously; but as to the conspirators, while expecting

ing Abellino's appearance, they suffered the torments of the damned.

Grave and tranquil sat the Doge in his chair, like a judge appointed to pass sentence on this King of the Banditti. The spectators stood around in various groupes, all hushed and solemn as were they waiting to receive their final judgement. The lovely Rosabella, with all the security of angels, whose innocence have nothing to fear, reclined her head on Camilla's shoulder, and gazed on her heroic lover with looks of adoration. The conspirators, with pallid cheeks and staring eyes, filled up the back-ground; and a dead and awful silence prevailed through the assembly, scarcely interrupted by a single breath!

—" And

—" And now then," said Flodoardo, " prepare yourselves, for this terrible Abellino shall immediately appear before you! Do not tremble; he shall do no one harm."—

With these words he turned away from the company, and advanced towards the folding-doors; he paused for a few moments, and concealed his face in his cloak.

—" Abellino!" cried he at length, raising his head, and extending his arm towards the door.—At that name all who heard it shuddered involuntarily, and Rosabella advanced unconsciously a few steps towards her lover. She trembled at the Bravo's approach, yet trembled more for Flodoardo than herself.

—" Abellino!"

—" Abellino!" the Florentine repeated in a loud and angry tone, threw from him his mantle and barrette, and had already laid his hand on the lock of the door to open it, when Rosabella uttered a cry of terror!"—

—" Stay, Flodoardo!" she cried, rushing towards him, and.... Ha! Flodoardo was gone, and there, in his place, stood Abellino, and shouted out—" Ho! ho!"—

CHAP. VI.

Apparitions.

INSTANTLY a loud cry of terror resounded through the apartment. Rosabella sank fainting at the Bravo's feet; the conspirators were almost suffocated with rage, terror, and astonishment, the ladies made signs of the cross, and began in all haste to repeat their paternosters; the senators stood rooted to their places like so many statues, and the

the Doge doubted the information of his ears and eyes.

Calm and terrible stood the Bravo before them, in all the pomp of his strange and awful ugliness; with his Bravo's habit, his girdle filled with pistols and poniards, his distorted yellow countenance, his black and bushy eye-brows, his lips convulsed, his right eye covered by a large patch, and his left half buried among the wrinkles of flesh which swelled around it. He gazed round him for a few moments in silence, and then approached the stupefied Andreas.

—" Ho! ho!" he roared in a voice like thunder, " you wished to see the bravo Abellino?—Doge of Venice, here he he stands, and is come to claim his bride!"—

Andreas gazed with looks of horror on this model for demons, and at length stammered out with difficulty —" It cannot be real! I must surely be the sport of some terrible dream!"—

—" Without there! Guards!" exclaimed the Cardinal Gonzaga, and would have hastened to the folding-doors; when Abellino put his back against them, snatched a pistol from his girdle, and pointed it at the Cardinal's bosom.

—" The first," cried he, " who calls for the guard, or advances one step from the place on which he stands, expires that

that moment—Fools! Do ye think, I would have delivered myself up, and desired that guards might beset these doors, had I feared their swords, or intended to escape from your power?—No! I am content to be your prisoner, but not through compulsion! I am content to be your prisoner, and it was with that intent that I came hither. No mortal should have the glory of seizing Abellino; if justice required him to be delivered up, it was necessary that he should be delivered up by *himself!*—Or do ye take Abellino for an ordinary ruffian, who passes his time in skulking from the sbirri, and who murders for the sake of despicable plunder? No, by heaven, no! Abellino was no such common villain!—It's true I was a Bravo;

but

but the motives which induced me to become one were great and striking!"

Andreas—[clasping his hands together]—Almighty God! can all this be possible!

An awful silence again reigned through the saloon. All trembled while they listened to the voice of the terrible assassin, who strode through the chamber proud and majestic as the monarch of the infernal world.

Rosabella opened her eyes; their first look fell upon the Bravo.

—" Oh! God of mercy!" she exclaimed, " he is still there!—Methought too that Flodoardo.... No, no; it could
not

not be! I was deceived by witchcraft!"—

Abellino advanced towards her, and attempted to raise her. She shrunk from his touch with horror.

—" No, Rosabella," said the Bravo in an altered voice, " what you saw was no illusion. Your favoured Flodoardo is no other than Abellino, the Bravo."—

—" It is false!" interrupted Rosabella, starting from the ground in despair, and throwing herself for refuge on Camilla's bosom. " Monster, thou canst not be Flodoardo! such a fiend can never have been such a seraph!— Flodoardo's actions were good and glorious as a demi-god's! 'twas of him that I learnt

I learnt to love good and glorious actions, and 'twas he who encouraged me to attempt them myself! His heart was pure from all mean passions, and capable of conceiving all great designs! Never did he scruple in the cause of virtue to endure fatigue and pain: and to dry up the tears of suffering innocence .... that was Flodoardo's proudest triumph!—Flodoardo and *thou*......! Wretch, whom many a bleeding ghost has long since accused before the throne of Heaven, dare not thou to prophane the name of Flodoardo.

Abellino—[proud and earnest]—Rosabella, wilt thou forsake me? Wilt thou retract thy promise? Look, Rosabella, and be convinced: I, the Bravo, and thy Flodoardo are the same!"—

He said, removed the patch from his eye, and passed an handkerchief over his face once or twice; in an instant his complexion was altered, his bushy eyebrows and straight black hair disappeared, his features were replaced in their natural symmetry, and lo! the handsome Florentine stood before the whole assembly, drest in the habit of the bravo Abellino.

Abellino—Mark me, Rosabella! Seven times over, and seven times again, will I change my appearance, even before your eyes, and that so artfully, that study me as you will the transformation shall still deceive you—But change as I may, of one thing be assured; *I* am the man whom you loved as Flodoardo."—

The

The Doge gazed and listened without being able to recover from his confusion; but every now and then the words—"Dreadful! dreadful!" escaped from his lips, and he wrang his hands in agony. Abellino approached Rosabella, and said in the tone of supplication—"Rosabella, wilt thou break thy promise? Am I no longer dear to thee?"—

Rosabella was unable to answer; she stood like one changed to a statue, and fixed her motionless eyes on the Bravo.

Abellino took her cold hand, and prest it to his lips.

—"Rosabella," said he, "art thou still mine?"—

Rosabella—Flodoardo.... Oh! that I had never loved.... had never seen thee!

Abellino—Rosabella, wilt thou still be the bride of Flodoardo?—wilt thou be " the Bravo's bride?"

Love struggled with abhorrence in Rosabella's bosom, and painful was the contest.

Abellino—Hear me, beloved-one! It was for thee that I have discovered myself.... that I have delivered myself into the hands of justice! For thee.... Oh! what would I not do for thee!—Rosabella, I wait but to hear one syllable from your lips! speak but a decisive
" yes!"

"yes!" or "no!" and all is ended!—Rosabella, dost thou love me still?

And still she answered not; but she threw upon him a look innocent and tender as ever beamed from the eye of an angel, and that look betrayed but too plainly that the miscreant was still master of her heart. She turned from him hastily, threw herself into Camilla's arms, and exclaimed—" God forgive you, man, for torturing me so cruelly!"—

The Doge had by this time recovered from his stupor: he started from his chair; threats flashed from his eyes, and his lip trembled with passion—He rushed towards Abellino; but the senators threw themselves in his passage, and held him back by force. In the mean while the Bravo advanced towards him with the most insolent composure, and requested him to calm his agitation.

" Doge of Venice," said he, " will you keep your promise? That you gave it to me, these noble lords and ladies can testify!"—

Andreas—Monster! miscreant!—oh! how artfully has this plan been laid to ensnare me!—Tell me, Venetians; to *such* a creditor am I obliged to discharge my fearful debt?—Long has he been playing a deceitful, bloody part; the bravest of our citizens have fallen beneath his dagger, and it was the price of their blood which has enabled him to act the nobleman in Venice. Then comes he to me in the disguise of a man

of

of honour, seduces the heart of my unfortunate Rosabella, obtains my promise by an artful trick, and now claims the maiden for his bride, in the hope that the husband of the Doge's niece will easily obtain an absolution for his crimes. Tell me, Venetians, ought I to keep my word with this miscreant?

All the Senators—No! no! by no means!

Abellino—[with solemnity]—If you have once pledged your word, you ought to keep it, though given to the Prince of Darkness. Oh! fye, fye! Abellino, how shamefully hast thou been deceived in thy reckoning!—I thought I had to do with men of honour! Oh! how grossly have I been mistaken—[in a terrible

rible voice]—Once again, and for the last time, I ask you, Doge of Venice, wilt thou break thy princely word?"—

Andreas—[in the tone of authority]—Give up your arms?

Abellino—And you will really withhold from me my just reward?—Shall it be in vain that I delivered Abellino into your power?

Andreas—It was to the brave Flodoardo that I promised Rosabella; I never entered into an engagement with the murderer Abellino—Let Flodoardo claim my niece, and she is his; but Abellino can have no claim to her. Again I say lay down your arms.

Abellino

Abellino—[laughing wildly]—The murderer Abellino, say you? Ho! ho! Be it your care to keep your own promises, and trouble not yourself about my murders—they are *my* affair, and I warrant I shall find a word or two to say in defence of them when the judgment-day arrives.

Gonzaga—[to the Doge]—What dreadful blasphemy!

Abellino—Oh! good Lord Cardinal, intercede in my behalf—You know me well; I have always acted by you like a man of honour, that at least you cannot deny!—Say a word in my favour then, good Lord Cardinal!

Gonzaga—[angrily, and with imperious

rious dignity]—Address not thyself to *me*, miscreant! What canst thou and I have to do together?—Venerable Andreas, delay no longer; let the guards be called in!

Abellino—What? Is there then no hope for me?—Does no one feel compassion for the wretched Abellino?—What? *no one!*—[a pause]—All are silent!—*all!*—'Tis enough! Then my fate is decided—Call in your guards!

Rosabella—[with a scream of agony springing forward, and falling at the Doge's feet]—Mercy! mercy!—Pardon him.... pardon *Abellino!*

Abellino—[in rapture]—Say'st thou so?

so?—Ho! ho! then an angel prays for Abellino in his last moments!

Rosabella — [clasping the Doge's knees]—Have mercy on him, my friend! my father!—He is a sinner......but leave him to the justice of Heaven!—He is a sinner......but oh! Rosabella loves him still.

Andreas—[pushing her away with indignation]—Away, unworthy girl! you rave!

Abellino folded his arms, gazed with eagerness on what was passing, and tears gushed into his brilliant eyes. Rosabella caught the Doge's hand, as he turned to leave her, kist it twice, and said—" If you have no mercy on *him*, then have none

none on *me!* The sentence which you pass on Abellino will be mine; 'tis for my own life that I plead as well as Abellino's; Father! dear father! reject not my suit, but spare him!

Andreas—[in an angry and decided tone]—Abellino dies!

Abellino—And can you look on with dry eyes while that innocent dove bleeds at your feet? Go, barbarian; you never loved Rosabella as she deserved: now is she yours no longer! She is mine, she is Abellino's!"—

He raised her from the ground, and prest her pale lips against his own.

—" Rosabella, thou art mine; death alone

alone parts us! thou lov'st me as I *would* be loved; I am blest, whate'er may happen, and can now set fortune at defiance—To business then!"—

He replaced Rosabella, who was almost fainting, on the bosom of Camilla, then advanced into the middle of the chamber, and addrest the assembly with an undaunted air:

—" Venetians, you are determined to deliver me up to the axe of justice! there is for me no hope of mercy! 'Tis well! act as you please; but ere you sit in judgment over *me*, Signors, I shall take the liberty of passing sentence upon some few of *you!* Now mark me! you see in me the murderer of Conari! the murderer of Paolo Manfrone! the murderer

murderer of Lomellino! I deny it not! But would you know the illustrious persons who payed me for the use of my dagger...."—

With these words he put a whistle to his lips, sounded it, and instantly the doors flew open, the guards rushed in, and ere they had time to recollect themselves, the chief conspirators were in custody, and disarmed.

—" Guard them well!" said Abellino in a terrible voice to the sentinels; " you have your orders!—Noble Venetians, look on these villains; it is to them that you are indebted for the loss of your three noblest citizens! I accuse of those murders, one, two, three, four, ...and

.... and my good Lord Cardinal there has the honour to be the fifth."—

Motionless and bewildered stood the accused; tale-telling confession spoke in every feature that the charge was true, and no one was bold enough to contradict Abellino.

—" What can all this mean ?" asked the senators of each other, in the utmost surprize and confusion.

—" This is all a shameful artifice," the Cardinal at length contrived to say; " the villain, perceiving that he has no chance of escaping punishment, is willing, out of mere resentment, to involve *us* in his destruction."—

Contarino—[recovering himself]—In the wickedness of his life he has surpast all former miscreants, and now he is trying to surpass them in the wickedness of his death.

Abellino—[with majesty]—Be silent!—I know your whole plot, have seen your list of proscriptions, am well informed of your whole arrangement, and at the moment that I speak to you, the officers of justice are employed by my orders in seizing the gentlemen with the white ribands round their arms, who this very night intended to overturn Venice—Be silent, for defence were vain.

Andreas—[in astonishment]—Abellino, what is the meaning of all this?

Abellino

the honour of your wives from the pollutor's kiss, and the throats of your innocent children from the knife of the assassin.... Men! men! and yet will you send me to the scaffold?

Look on this list! See how many among you would have bled this night, had it not been for Abellino, and see where the miscreants stand by whom you would have bled!—Read you not in every feature, that they are already condemned by heaven and their own conscience? Does a single mouth unclose itself in exculpation? Does a single movement of the head give the lie to my charge? Yet the truth of what I have advanced shall be made still more evident.—

He turned himself to the conspirators.

—" Mark me!" said he, " the first among you who acknowledges the truth, shall receive a free pardon. I swear it, *I*, the Bravo Abellino!"—

The conspirators remained silent— Suddenly Memmo started forward, and threw himself trembling at the Doge's feet.

— " Venetians!" he exclaimed, " Abellino has told you true!"—

—" 'Tis false! 'tis false!" exclaimed the accused all together.

—" Silence!" cried Abellino in a voice

Abellino—Neither more nor less than that Abellino has discovered and defeated a conspiracy against the constitution of Venice and the life of its Doge! The Bravo, in return for your kind intention of sending him to destruction in a few hours, has preserved you from it.

Vitalba—[to the accused]—Noble Venetians, you are silent under this heavy charge.

Abellino—They are wise, for no defence could now avail them. Their troops are already disarmed, and lodged in separate dungeons of the state-prison: visit them there, and you will learn more. You now understand probably that I did not order the doors of this saloon to be guarded for the purpose of seizing the terrible Bravo Abellino, but of taking those heroes into secure custody.

And now, Venetians, compare together *your* conduct and *mine!* At the hazard of my life have I preserved the state from ruin; disguised as a Bravo, I dared to enter the assembly of those ruthless villains whose daggers laid Venice waste; I have endured for your sakes storm, and rain, and frost, and heat; I have watched for your safety while ye were sleeping; Venice owes to my care her constitution and your lives; and yet are my services deserving of no reward?—All this have I done for Rosabella of Corfu, and yet will you withhold from me my promised bride? I have saved you from death, have saved the

voice of thunder, while the indignation which flamed in every feature struck terror into his hearers; " silence, I say, and hear me—or rather hear the ghosts of your victims!—Appear! appear!" cried this dreadful man in a tone still louder, " 'tis time!"—

Again he sounded his whistle; the folding-doors were thrown open, and there stood the Doge's so much lamented friends Conari, Lomellino, and Manfrone!

—" We are betrayed!" shouted Contarino, drew out a concealed dagger, and plunged it in his bosom up to the very hilt.

And now what a scene of rapture followed.

lowed. Tears streamed down the silver beard of Andreas as he rushed into the arms of his long-lost companions: tears bedewed the cheeks of the venerable triumvirate, as they once more clasped the knees of their prince, their friend, their brother! These excellent men, these heroes, never had Andreas hoped to meet them again till they should meet in Heaven; and Andreas blest Heaven for permitting him to meet them once more on earth. Those four men, who had valued each other in the first dawn of *youth*, who had fought by each other's sides in *manhood*, were now assembled in *age*, and valued each other more than ever!—The spectators gazed with universal interest on the scene before them, and the good old senators mingled tears of joy with those shed by the re-united companions.

companions. In the happy delirium of this moment nothing but Andreas and his friends was attended to: no one was aware that the conspirators and the self-murderer Contarino were removed by the guards from the saloon; no one but Camilla observed Rosabella, who threw herself sobbing on the bosom of the handsome Bravo, and repeated a thousand times—" Abellino then is not a murderer!"—

At length they began to recollect themselves—they looked round them—and the first words which broke from every lip were—" Hail, saviour of Venice!"—The roof rang with the name of Abellino, and unnumbered blessings accompanied the name.

That

That very Abellino, who not an hour before had been doomed to the scaffold by the whole assembly, now stood calm and dignified as a god before the adoring spectators; and now he viewed with complacency the men whose lives he had saved, and now his eye dwelt with rapture on the woman whose love was the reward of all his dangers.

—" Abellino!" said Andreas, advancing to the Bravo, and extending his hand towards him.

—" I am not Abellino," replied he smiling, while he prest the Doge's hand respectfully to his lips, " neither am I Flodoardo of Florence. I am by birth a Neapolitan, and by name Rosalvo: the death of my inveterate enemy the
Prince

Prince of Monaldeschi makes it no longer necessary to conceal who I really am."—

—" Monaldeschi?" repeated Andreas with a look of anxiety.

—" Fear not!" continued Rosalvo; " Monaldeschi, it's true, fell by my hand, but fell in honourable combat. The blood which stained his sword flowed from my veins, and in his last moments conscience asserted her empire in his bosom. He died not till he had written in his tablets the most positive declaration of my innocence as to the crimes with which his hatred had contrived to blacken me; and he also instructed me by what means I might obtain at Naples the restoration of my forfeited estates

and

and the re-establishment of my injured honour. Those means have been already efficacious, and all Naples is by this time informed of the arts by which Monaldeschi procured my banishment, and of the many plots which he laid for my destruction; plots, which made it necessary for me to drop my own character, and never to appear but in disguise. After various wanderings, chance led me to Venice; my appearance was so much altered, that I dreaded not discovery, but I dreaded [and with reason] perishing in your streets with hunger. In this situation accident brought me acquainted with the banditti, by whom Venice was then infested; I willingly united myself to their society, partly with the view of purifying the republic from the presence of these wretches,

and

and partly in the hope of discovering through them the more illustrious villains, by whom their daggers were employed. I was successful; I delivered the banditti up to justice, and stabbed their captain in Rosabella's sight. I was now the only Bravo in Venice; every scoundrel was obliged to have recourse to me; I discovered the plans of the conspirators, and now *you* know them also. I found that the deaths of the Doge's three friends had been determined on; and in order to obtain full confidence with the confederates, it was necessary to persuade them that these men had fallen beneath my dagger. No sooner had my plan been formed, than I imparted it to Lomellino; he, and he *only* was my confidant in this business. He presented me to the Doge as the
son

son of a deceased friend; he assisted me with his advice; he furnished me with keys to those doors to the public gardens which none were permitted to pass through except Andreas and his particular friends, and which frequently enabled me to elude pursuit; he showed me several private passages in the palace, by which I could penetrate unobserved even into the Doge's very bed-chamber; when the time for his disappearance arrived, he not only readily consented to lie concealed in a retreat known only to ourselves, but was also the means of inducing Manfrone and Conari to join him in his retirement, till the fortunate issue of this day's adventure permitted me to set them once more at liberty. The banditti exist no longer; the conspirators are in chains; my plans are accomplished;

accomplished; and now, Venetians, if you still think him deserving of it, here stands the Bravo Abellino, and you may lead him to the scaffold when you will!"—

—" To the scaffold?" exclaimed at once the Doge, the senators, and the whole crowd of nobili; and every one burst into enthusiastic praises of the dauntless Neapolitan.

—" Oh! Abellino," exclaimed Andreas while he wiped away a tear; " I would gladly give my ducal bonnet to be such a Bravo as thou hast been!— ' Doge,' didst thou once say to me, ' thou and I are the two greatest men in Venice'—but oh! how much greater is the Bravo than the Doge!—Rosabella

is

is that jewel, than which I have nothing in the world more precious; Rosabella is dearer to me than an emperor's crown; Rosabella is thine."—

—" Abellino!" said Rosabella, and extended her hand to the handsome Bravo.

—" Triumph!" cried he, " Rosabella is the Bravo's Bride!"—and he clasped the blushing maid to his bosom.

CHAP. VII.

Conclusion.

AND now it would be not at all amiss to make Count Rosalvo sit down quietly between the good old Doge and his lovely niece; and then cause him to relate the motive of Monaldeschi's hatred, in what manner he lost Valeria, what crimes were imputed to him, and how he escaped from the assassins sent in pursuit of him by his enemy; how he had long wandered from place to place, and how

how he had at length learnt [during his abode in Bohemia with a gang of gypsies] such means of disguising his features as enabled him to defy the keenest penetration to discover in the beggar Abellino the once-admired Count Rosalvo; how in this disguise he had returned to Italy; and how Lomellino, having ascertained that he was universally believed at Naples to have long since perished by shipwreck, [and therefore that neither the officers of the Inquisition nor the assassins of his enemy were likely to trouble themselves any more about him,] he had ventured to resume with some slight alterations his own appearance at Venice; how the arrival of Monaldeschi had obliged him to conceal himself, till an opportunity offered of presenting himself to the
Prince

Prince when unattended, and of demanding satisfaction for his injuries; how he had been himself wounded in several places by his antagonist, though the combat finally terminated in his favour; how he had resolved to make use of Monaldeschi's death to terrify Andreas still further, and of Parozzi's conspiracy to obtain Rosabella's hand of the Doge; how he had trembled lest the heart of his mistress should have been only captivated by the romantic appearance of the adventurer Flodoardo, and have rejected him when known to be the Bravo Abellino; how he had resolved to make use of the terror inspired by the assassin to put her love to the severest trial; and how, had she failed in that trial, he had determined to renounce the inconstant maid for ever; with many other *hows,*
whys.

whys, and *wherefores,* which not being explained will, I doubt, leave much of this tale still involved in mystery: but before I begin Rosalvo's history I must ask two questions—

First, Do my readers like the manner in which I relate adventures?

Secondly, If my readers *do* like my manner of relating adventures, can't I employ my time better than in relating them?

When these questions are answered, I may possibly resume my pen. In the mean while, Gentlemen and Ladies, good night, and pleasant dreams attend you!

FINIS.

ERRATA.

Page 49 line 8 *for* numbered *read* number
  66 — 8 omit the inflected commas
  90 — 14 *for* altar *read* altars
  100 — 4 *for* made *read* gave
  111 — 6 *for* nothing *read* nothing must be done
  ibid. — 8 *for* must do *read* must chuse
  120 — 9 *for* with mixture *read* with a mixture
  162 — 5 *for* laid down *read* imposed upon herself
  173 — 12 omit the second himself
  200 — 7 *for* all *read* well
  239 — 16 *for* unworthily *read* so unworthily
  273 — 4 *for* past *read* employed
  282 — 3 *Chamber* should not be in italics
  284 — 2 *for* the banditti *read* the Bravo
  314 — 6 *after* your arms put a full stop
  323 — 10 *after* charge put a note of interrogation

The Translator's absence from England while this Romance was publishing, must account for this long string of errata : fortunately there are few of sufficient consequence to make the meaning of any passage doubtful.

M. G. L.

SHURY, PRINTER.]

GOTHIC NOVELS

ARNO PRESS

in cooperation with

McGrath Publishing Company

Dacre, Charlotte ("Rosa Matilda"). **Confessions of the Nun of St. Omer,** A Tale. 2 vols. 1805. New Introduction by Devendra P. Varma.

Godwin, William. **St. Leon: A Tale of the Sixteenth Century.** 1831. New Foreword by Devendra P. Varma. New Introduction by Juliet Beckett.

Lee, Sophia. **The Recess: Or, A Tale of Other Times.** 3 vols. 1783. New Foreword by J. M. S. Tompkins. New Introduction by Devendra P. Varma.

Lewis, M[atthew] G[regory], trans. **The Bravo of Venice,** A Romance. 1805. New Introduction by Devendra P. Varma.

Prest, Thomas Preskett. **Varney the Vampire.** 3 vols. 1847. New Foreword by Robert Bloch. New Introduction by Devendra P. Varma.

Radcliffe, Ann. **The Castles of Athlin and Dunbayne: A Highland Story.** 1821. New Foreword by Frederick Shroyer.

Radcliffe, Ann. **Gaston De Blondeville.** 2 vols. 1826. New Introduction by Devendra P. Varma.

Radcliffe, Ann. **A Sicilian Romance.** 1821. New Foreword by Howard Mumford Jones. New Introduction by Devendra P. Varma.

Radcliffe, Mary-Anne. **Manfroné: Or The One-Handed Monk.** 2 vols. 1828. New Foreword by Devendra P. Varma. New Introduction by Coral Ann Howells.

Sleath, Eleanor. **The Nocturnal Minstrel.** 1810. New Introduction by Devendra P. Varma.